# Stuck in the Dark

# II

a novel

by
**GWEN CANNON**

## G PUBLISHING LLC

Detroit, Michigan

Edited by: Anthony Ambrogio

Cover Design: Iybe Media
Photo: Kennard LaJaun
Model: Jamey Kojima
Makeup: Raquel Franks
Published by G Publishing, LLC

ISBN 13: 978-0-9823533-9-4
ISBN 10: 0-9823533-9-1

Library of Congress Control Number: 2009909466
Printed in the United States of America

www.gwencannon.net

# Acknowledgements

Hello friends and family, words cannot begin to express how truly blessed I am. As I continue to tell a story through my books, I am encouraged by the love and support I receive from family and friends. As the saying goes, I have an awesome God, and I could not have made this journey with my books without his guidance and love. I have to give my love and deepest gratitude to my friend, lover, and husband, James Cannon. We've been through a lot over the years, and my love for you grows stronger every day. You're my Goliath—strong, powerful and full of wisdom. You pick me up when everything seems to be going wrong in my life. To my mother, Mary Collins: I'm blessed to have you in my life. I would like to send out a special thank you to Kim and Sherise Watkins, Tim and Darryln Ford. (Darrylyn, you continue to astonish me with your overwhelming support of my books; words cannot express how much I appreciate you.) To Ms. Nollie: you are crazzzyyy...; I love the motivation you have for my books. Thanks to Kim Tyler, my sister, my friend, my awesome stylist. Beautiful, artististic, and full of suprises....(Ms. Message Therapist), please don't give up doing my hair; I don't know what I would do. Thanks to my family, who continues to support me: My sisters Margie (and her husband, Kevin Tabb), Rosilin, Debra, and Rosemary; my brother, Aaron, and his wife, Lisa, in Atlanta; my nieces—Kesha,

Catrea, Reese, Jessica, Kaela, Brandie, and Tosha—and my nephew, Lamar. To my big sister Yvonne Burge, you have taken care of me in so many ways, I can't begin to express my gratitude and thanks. Jackie Harvard, my sister, my friend, we go back a long way. Thank you so much for your continued support. Thanks to the Cannon family—Fay, Delana, Nitra, Bryan, and his wife, Crystal—and to a host of friends who continue to show their support: Toyia Baker, Belinda Robinson, Emily Goodman, Gisela Estevan, Sam Garcia, Serena Levy, E'lois Thomas; Carla, Chili, Charles, and DeAnna Crump; David and Tajuana Warren, Coach Turner, Ing, Sylvester, Billie Schuh, Mr. and Mrs. Kevin Beal, Denise, Tiffany, Danyelle, Pat, Juanita Lomax, William Lomax. And as always a special thank you to my BFF, James and Lettice Crawford.

# Prologue

Nothing could prepare me for what happened next—the escalating sound of gunshots and screams could be heard throughout the house. I started running in the opposite direction of the gunfire. My only thought was to try to get the hell out there as fast as possible. But, before I could make it to the door, I felt an intense burning sensation. My back felt as if someone had taken a blow torch to it. I fell face forward on the floor.

I lay there with tears streaming down my face; I couldn't move. I felt as if a ton of bricks were stacked on top of my back. I could hear footsteps, coming closer and closer—a woman's footstep; I could tell by the heels tapping on the floor. I lay there, pretending to be dead.

As she walked around me, saying, "You little bitch," I could hear sirens in the distance; someone must have heard the commotion and called the police. *Please, Lord, hurry up, and let this bitch go on her way; I don't want to die.* It felt like hours, but I knew it only had been seconds stretching into minutes.

My back was soaking wet; I knew it was from my blood. How much was I losing? I didn't have a clue. I started feeling cold; I was losing consciousness.

As I lay there on the floor, I thought of all the shit I had tucked away in my closet, deep dark secrets no one even knew.

# Chapter 1

### Tina

Waiting to board my flight to New York, I reflected back on the last few months. The secrets that had surfaced about people I thought I knew.

My thoughts drifted back to Chris's funeral. It had been a cloudy, dreary day. I had never seen so much rain in my life. I thought it would never stop. I stood there at Chris's gravesite, holding on to Attorney Patton's hand. Tim, Lisa, and G attended the funeral services. Rock said there was no way he would attend the funeral, knowing what Chris had done to Tracy. I truly understood where Rock was coming from. I couldn't blame him for staying away.

It was impossible for me to forgive what Chris had done to Tracy, but the least I could do was pay my last respects. Chris and I had a history together; I still loved him and cared for him, but I was not in love with him.

Mark seemed to be taking it really hard. He kept breaking down, grabbing hold of the casket. I saw the way Chris's mother and father were looking at Mark. I knew they were wondering just what kind of friend Mark had been to their son.

I didn't realize Chris had so many friends. A lot of people showed up to pay their respects. I kept asking myself who these people were. They were mostly men. Nice looking brothers who definitely looked like they had money.

They all were dressed in expensive tailor made suits that wrapped their body to fit just right. Their shoes were Italian, Gucci, Prada's and Gator's. The cars they drove looked like they had just picked them up off the showroom floor. Yeah, whoever these gentlemen were, they definitely looked like they had it going on. I wanted to introduce myself, but I thought better of it. One man did stand out from the rest. Chris's mother kept hugging him. I wondered what his relationship was to Chris. Maybe he was a cousin or close friend of the family. I knew Chris had a younger sister and brother. Chris was the oldest.

His sister, Alexis had long black silky hair pulled back in a pony tail that showed her facial features really well. She could have easily passed for a model. She was about 5'9", and very shapely. She kept smiling at me. She was the only one who actually acknowledged me at the funeral. She came up to me and extended her hand, and introduced herself as Chris sister. She said that Chris always talked about me. She kept looking me up and down as if she was trying to see what Chris saw in me. Finally after physically analyzing my appearance, she told me I was prettier in person. I smiled and thanked her for her compliment and excused myself. I wasn't feeling her at all. What the fuck was she doing checking me out as if I was a nigga, and she had the audacity to be smiling at the same time. She really made me feel uncomfortable. Chris mother and father didn't utter a word when I walked up to them and extended my condolences. Again, I excused myself and made my way to the back of the church. I went looking for Attorney Patterson. I was ready to go.

As I was leaving coming down the church stairs, Chris younger brother Eric was standing outside. He refused to come in the church. He stood there the whole time the funeral was going on. I wasn't looking forward to another funeral, but I knew I had to pay my respects to Jason's woman, Monica. Her funeral was just as crowded as Chris's. I still can't believe that Mike was the one who shot her. What the fuck was he thinking? Now he's sitting in jail, about to do time for murder and, on top of that, the drug charges.

He's going to be there a long-ass time. Luckily Jason didn't tell the police that Mike had shot *him* too, or Mike would be doing even more time. They gave him 25 years to life, he goes up for parole in 30. Damn, he has fucked up his life for real. That shit we do in the dark will bite us in the ass eventually.

"Please have your boarding pass ready when you approach the entrance," said the flight attendant, waking me up out of my trance. "Welcome aboard Northern Airlines; I hope you enjoy your flight."

"Thank you," I said and went to look for my assigned seat.

*I better get my ass back in gear and stop thinking about shit that's in the past. I need to move on with my life. This trip is exactly what I need. I was glad when I received a call from Macy's New York buyer, whom I had contacted over a month ago to inquire about being their client. I knew, if I became a regular client, I could get merchandise for my store at the merchant wholesale price.*

*Damn, I hope I'm not sitting next to someone who's going to talk the whole damn flight. I wanted to get in a little nap before we landed.*

*Just my luck, I'm sitting next to a woman. I hope she keeps her mouth shut. I don't feel like being friendly today. As luck would have it, I'm stuck in the middle seat. My mouth almost dropped to the floor when I looked up to see who was making his way to my row.*

# Chapter 2

## Tracy

"Tracy, baby how you feeling today?" asked Rock, getting up out of the bed.

"Much better. My headaches come and go, but I'll be all right,"

"Well, I'm going to the gym to get my work out on. I've been packing on the pounds in the last couple of weeks" said Rock, strutting around the room patting his stomach.

"Baby, you look good to me." I smiled.

"Yeah, right," laughed Rock, looking at himself in the mirror.

"Come here, baby; let me see your six pack."

Rock walked over to me and lifted up his shirt. I stuck my hands down his boxers and said, "Your pack feels okay to me."

"Damn baby, see what you did!" said Rock, pointing to the erection in his boxers.

"Well, then, let momma take care of big daddy."

"Are you sure you're up to this baby?" asked Rock, looking concerned.

"My head was injured, not my Poonanny, baby, and it's been a while. We still haven't consummated our wedding vows like we should have," I smiled, undressing, all the while looking at Rock's reaction.

Rock stood there watching as I undressed. His erection was standing at attention, ready for combat. He couldn't get his clothes off fast enough. It had been weeks; Just the thought of making love had his dick throbbing wanting to bust a nut. I couldn't take my eyes off his dick, it was as if I was in a trance. At that moment I just wanted to feel him inside of me. I walked over to Rock and started stroking his penis. He gently put my breast in his mouth and starting a slow sucking motion, the sensation was driving me crazy. With a smooth motion of his hand, he put his middle index finger gently in my vagina and started rubbing my clit. I threw my head back, moaning for more. Ohhh.....

"Damn, baby, your pussy feels so good."

Rock slowly picked me up; I knew he wanted to take his time so as not to hurt me.

"Baby, I'm not going to break. It's all right." I pulled him on top of me, just the feel of his penis rubbing against my leg had my pussy throbbing, wanting his dick inside of me. I couldn't wait any longer, I slowly took his penis and guided it inside me.

"Mmmh! *Damn*, baby, your dick feels so good!" I moaned.

"I don't want to hurt you, baby," moaned Rock in turn as he kept up a slow, rhythmic stroke while sucking on my nipples.

"Oh, *yes!*" I cried, holding onto Rock.

"Damn, baby, you don't know how much I missed your pussy. It's so *hot!*" Rock cried in turn, clutching my buttocks.

"Baby, don't stop!" I screamed.

But Rock couldn't hold back; he exploded all over me. The cum was dripping from his penis, onto my thigh.

Gwen Cannon

"Damn, baby, you couldn't' wait for me?" I was upset. It had been months since I had some dick and this motherfucka came in less than five minutes. Hell yeah, I was upset. I got up from the bed trying not to show my disappointment. I had got all built up in the heat of the moment and his ass couldn't wait to bust a nut.

"Baby, I tried! I couldn't hold back. You know it's been a while," As he laid there panting from letting go what he had built up inside of him over the months.

"Nigga, you know you gone have to take care of a sister." I spread my thighs and pointed to my vagina.

Rock threw my legs over his shoulders and started licking my clit, doing his best to give me an orgasm. I didn't have to tell him that he was licking the right spot—he knew from my grunts and moans of pleasure that he was taking care of his baby. My pussy was throbbing, about to explode.

"Yeah baby, right there, yes, ohh....!"

I moved my pelvis in unison with Rock's tongue, grabbing a hold of his bald head. I was holding on for dear life, afraid if I let go, I would lose his rhythm. I could feel my toes curling, balling up tightly until I could feel the orgasm I wanted so bad explode into Rock's mouth.

"Yes, YES!" I shouted, my orgasm dripping from me, leg shaking from the orgasmic climax I had just experienced.

I lay across the bed, eyes closed, with a smile of pleasure plastered across my face. Rock had accomplished what he set out to do. He hated whenever he couldn't bring me to a climax, but he always made up for it later. He knew how to please a woman in the bed. He got up and went into the bathroom. I could hear the sound of brushing teeth and gargling. He stood in the doorway of the bathroom smiling to himself. I knew what he was thinking: *Yeah, I knocked her ass right the fuck out.*

"Baby, you better hurry up and get your work out on. You know I have an appointment today with Dr. Jones, and I have my therapy treatment at 4:00 o'clock," I reminded him.

"Damn, you were just snoring a minute ago," said Rock. "Where'd you get that burst of energy from?"

"I'm straight now," I said. To prove it, I jumped up out of the bed and pranced around the room naked.

"Baby, you sexy as hell!"

"You like?" I purred seductively, sidling up to him.

"I *like...*" Rock emphasized, as if this were the first time he'd seen me naked.

I pushed him away. "Take your ass to the gym before it's too late."

"Okay. I'll be back in time to take you to your appointment, though."

"I can't wait until Tina gets back in town. Damn, I miss my girl," I confessed.

"She needed to get away for a while," said Rock.

"I know. She's been through a lot these last few months."

"I know for a fact that Tina is a true friend. She was by your side the whole time you were in the hospital. I had to make her ass go home and brush her teeth," said Rock.

"Don't be talking about my girl," I mockingly threatened.

"You didn't smell her breath," laughed Rock.

"Now, get your ass to the gym, before it's too late..." I pushed him out the door.

"Okay, okay, I'll see you in an hour," Rock promised, walking toward the car.

# Chapter 3

## Jason

*D*amn, I don't know if I want to go visit Mike today. I know I promised him, I would come, but I don't like seeing my brother locked up. He has done some fucked-up shit in the last few months. Killing my girl Monica, getting caught up with drugs, and shooting me. I know he didn't mean to shoot me. That's why I told the cops I didn't know who shot me. But Monica—damn, that's a hard pill to swallow. I miss the hell out of Monica, but ol' girl at the hospital been keeping my mind occupied. I know it's only been a few months, but I have to move on. I know Monica would want me to. Maybe I should stop by the hospital and pay Doctor Jones *a visit. She keeps playing hard to get, but I know she's feeling me. I haven't been out lately, either. I thought about going down to Shake that Ass, but it will bring back too many memories. I'm bored as hell. I'll call Rock and G and see what's up for tonight.*

\*\*\*\*\*\*\*\*\*\*\*\*\*\*\*\*\*\*\*\*\*\*\*\*\*\*\*\*\*\*\*\*\*\*

*Come on G, answer the damn phone, nigga.*

"Hello," said G.

"Damn, man, were you still asleep? It's almost one o'clock," I said.

"I was out late last night? said G, yawning into the phone.

"On a Thursday?" I asked him.

"Yeah, I was down at Shake that Ass."

"My ol' spot," I laughed.

"Yeah, they got new shit up in there. The females are the shit," said G.

"I didn't even know you liked the strip clubs."

"Lately, that's where I've been spending my time," G admitted.

"I hope you ain't been spending all your money up in there."

"Hell naw," said G.

"Must be some female up in there you like," I suggested.

"Yeah, this broad named Nicky," G confessed. "She tight as hell."

"Oh, it's like that." I was concerned. "Don't get caught up in no shit with a stripper. You see what happened to my brother, and my girl Monica."

"Oh, hell naw. It's ain't like that. Just hit it and quit," said G. Even through the phone, I could tell he was smiling.

"Don't hit some shit you can't shake, bro. Make sure you strapping up," I advised.

"For sho..." said G.

"I wanted to kill Monica when I saw her up in there," I told him, thinking back to when I went to Shake that Ass and saw Monica performing. But the thought of her made me grin, just the same.

"Yeah, I'm sorry about what happened to her, man," G comisserated. "You seem to be coming along okay."

"Yeah, I gotta move on with my life. I'm still young."

"Well, what you got up for tonight?" asked G.

"I don't know. I thought about going to the Back Door Bar for a minute. Maybe you, me, Rock, and Tim can meet up later. We haven't been out together in a while."

"That's straight," said G.

"I'll holla at Rock and Tim, see if they can get out. Married men gotta check in with the wifey," I laughed.

"Yeah," G agreed. "I never thought Rock would get married. I guess, when he thought Tracy wasn't going to make it, that shit made him change his mind. I think that nigga still out there fucking around, though."

"He's married," I protested.

"That don't mean shit to Rock. I knew that nigga back in the day. He used to be a straight-up ho'. Banging any broad that would open her legs. I don't know if he's changed since that incident with Tracy. He took an oath to honor and obey. Marriage shouldn't be taken lightly. You stand before God and give your vow to be faithful, and stand by your wife. —That's why I'm not ready yet."

"I was ready. Monica was my boo."

"Yeah, Monica was trying to do something with her life," G approved. "Going to college and shit."

"I know. I just lost it when I saw her shaking her ass at that club."

"I know she probably was about to shit on herself when she saw you," said G, laughing.

"Yeah, that shit was funny as hell. You should have seen her face. Hey, I better call them nigga's before it gets too late. Their wives probably have their day already planned out."

"Tracy got that nigga Rock on lock down," said G.

"I'm glad she's doing okay now. That was some fucked up shit Chris did." I shook my head.

"Yeah, we thought we knew that nigga. But he had ghosts in his closet we didn't know about," said G.

"Everybody done did some shit they didn't want to come out, but that down-low shit—you don't play with that. You need to be up front about something like that. We still don't know who the fuck shot and killed him right in the courthouse. Whoever that motherfucka was, he or she didn't give a fuck. I thought it was Rock," I told G, "but I know he wouldn't do some shit like that. He don't have it in him."

"Yeah, that ain't Rock," G concurred.

"Well," I sighed, "I'll holla at Rock and Tim. What time you want to meet up?"

"About nine or ten," said G.

"Okay, I'll see you then." I hung up the phone.

# Chapter 4

## Tina

No this nigga ain't about to sit next to me. I know I said I was not going to dwell on that shit I walked in on, but I didn't think I would have to be around him.

"Hello, Tina," said Mark smiling.

"Hey," I muttered, not wanting to look at him.

"How have you been?" asked Mark. At least the nigga felt uncomfortable as well. I could tell.

"How in the hell did we end up on the same flight, and sitting in the same row, you stalking me?" I asked, still not making eye contact with Mark.

"If you want me to ask the stewardess if there's another seat, I can," said Mark trying not to be confrontational. *At least he's trying to keep peace with me.*

"No, it's okay, sit down. We're adults; we have to talk eventually. Let's just let the past be the past," I told him, trying to be okay with the situation.

Anyone walking past could tell there was so much tension in the air between the two of us you could cut it with a knife. Finally the passenger on the other side of me decided to make conversation with us both.

"You two know each other?" asked the woman, smiling.

"Yes." I tried to keep my conversation short. *Maybe she'll get the hint that I don't want to talk.*

"That's cool. I wish someone I knew was on the same flight as me. These flights can be boring as hell," she babbled—not taking the hint.

"Mark, why don't we switch seats?" I asked, doing a lousy job of hiding my annoyance.

"Okay." Mark figured out what I wanted—that I didn't want to be conversing with a total stranger. I'll give him credit for that; he knew me from when we dated; he knew I was not the friendliest person when it came to dealing with strangers.

The other passenger finally caught on once Mark and I switched seats. She turned up her nose and rolled her eyes at me and started reading a magazine.

*I hope and pray Mark don't start that apologetic shit. I don't want to go there anymore. I'm trying to let that shit die. I'm going to close my eyes and try to go to sleep.*

********************************

I woke up to female laughter. *No, this dumb broad ain't sitting up here having a friendly conversation with Mark, like she knows him, and his ass being just as friendly!*

Mark instantly stopped talking when he noticed me looking at him like he was crazy. He tried to play the shit off, telling ol' girl, "I better catch up on my work. I don't want to fall behind. I said I was going to get some done on the flight to New York." He pulled out his laptop.

"No problem. Thanks for keeping me company," said the passenger, smiling at him, then rolling her eyes at me.

I can get ghetto with the best of them. I wanted to say, "Bitch, he don't want you; he's *gay*." But, that's not me. I just wanted this flight to be over with. *Thirty more minutes, and we will be landing.* I couldn't wait, I better check on Tracy once I get to my hotel. I know her spoiled ass—probably driving Rock crazy. He has been so supportive of her, taking care of my girl since the incident with Chris. I have a lot of respect for him. Getting married to her right there in her hospital bed. That's love.

"Sir, can I get you anything?" asked the stewardess

"No, I'm okay." Mark flashed his winning smile at her. "These young ladies may want something, though."

I knew ol' girl, with her ghetto ass, was going to remark—and she did.

"How come you only asked him if he needed anything?" she accused the stewardess. "He's not the only one sitting here."

"I'm sorry, ma'am," the stewardess apologized, rolling her eyes. "May I get you anything?"

"Hell naw, bitch. Now take your ass back to work," said the passenger, crossing her arms across her chest.

The stewardess strutted off down the aisle, mumbling something under her breath. I could have sworn I heard her call ol' girl a ghetto bitch. Now that shit was entertaining, and funny as hell.

26          Gwen Cannon

The females on this flight seemed to be swarming like bees to Mark. *I have counted five different women so far, who have made it known that they are checking him out. He's definitely a handsome brother, and got it going on. I wonder if he's still dancing. I had heard that he stopped. I'll make a point to ask him before we land.*

"Thanks, Mark, for switching seats," I told him.

"You're welcome," smiled Mark, glad to receive a welcoming response from Tina.

"So, what have you been up to lately?" asked Tina

"I started modeling. That's why I'm going to New York." He seemed pleased that I was talking to him.

"That's great. I'm happy for you. I always used to tell you that you looked like those models in the magazines." Yeah, he was handsome as hell, with a tight as body. His abs along would make any woman tear her damn panties off.

"I see that you are still busy as ever," said Mark.

"Yeah, you know me. Can't seem to sit my ass still for too long."

"Well, I know I might be asking too much," Mark began tentatively, "but, if you get time while you're in New York, maybe we could have lunch or dinner." He looked anxiously for a response.

I don't know if I was enjoying our conversation or not, but before I knew it, I blurted out, "That would be great."

"Great! Here's my card. Call me and let me know what's good for you. I'll be in town for a week," said Mark.

"Okay."

"Please take your seats and fasten your seat belts; we will be landing at LaGuardia in ten minutes," the pilot announced over the intercom.

*About damn time, I'm exhausted. I can't wait to get checked into my hotel and take my ass to bed. I'll check in with Tracy tomorrow.*

# Chapter 5

## Tracy

"Rock, you can just drop me off," I said, getting out of the car. "I know you don't feel like sitting in the waiting room for me. I'll probably be here a couple of hours. I have physical therapy after I see Dr. Jones."

"Okay, Tracy, that's straight. I have to take care of some business, anyway. Call me when you're ready," said Rock.

"I'm always ready!" I said, reaching into the car and grabbing Rock's crotch.

"Your ass know you horny as hell. Must be that medication," Rock said.

"I don't need medication to be horny. I told you it's been a while. Just be ready when we get home."

"Is that a promise or a warning?"

"You'll see," I said closing the door.

Rock blew his horn and pulled away.

*I wonder if Dr. Thomas will be giving me my therapy treatment today? I've never been attracted to white guys, but he's got it going on, and his body—Oh, my God! I know his ass must be in the gym everyday. I'm sure the sistas would agree. He's definitely eye candy. He reminds me of Halle Berry's baby daddy. Excuse my language but that man is fine as hell. Damn, here comes Dr. Thomas now.*

********************************

"Hello Tracy, will I be seeing you today?" asked Dr. Thomas, smiling to cover up the fact that he was undressing me with his eyes.

I wish I could have told him I didn't mind. *You can see me whenever you want.*

"Yes, my appointment is at 4:00. I'll see you then," I said with a smirk I couldn't hide.

"You look nice today," he complimented me.

"Thank you," I said shyly. I couldn't avoid blushing.

"Okay, then, I guess I'll see you later," said Dr. Thomas, walking away.

*Damn, I don't know what it is about him, but he definitely makes a sister want to go to the other side of the fence. I better stop letting curiosity get to me. I almost got in trouble with my last boss, Mr. Ward. He wanted to schedule a fuck date for every Friday. That shit was fucked up. I just wanted to test the waters and see if he could fuck. Just thinking about that shit makes me laugh, with his wrinkly ass dick. I knew I couldn't go back to work there, not after that shit.*

"Mrs. Johnson, Dr. Jones is ready to see you now. Please go to room two," the nurse told me.

*I hope she gives me a clean bill of health. I'm ready to get back to work. I enjoy being at home, but it can get boring as hell. Plus, I need money if I want to go shopping. I haven't been in a while. My girl Tina did hook me up with some cute outfits she picked up the last time she was in New York. I hope she hook a sista up again.*

"So, how's my patient doing today?" asked Dr. Jones flipping through my file.

"I feel good—just slight headaches every now and then."

"That's normal because of the trauma to your head. Well, everything looks good the x-rays came back okay. I guess I can give you a clean bill of health to return back to work." said Dr. Jones. "—But I don't want you to do anything stressful," she added.

"Thanks. That's what I wanted to hear. Now all I have to do is find a job," I smiled.

"I want you to continue with your therapy treatments for another month, but you still should be okay to go back to work—that is, once you find employment," Dr. Jones smiled back at me.

"That shouldn't be a problem. For the last two weeks I have been applying online for jobs and sending out my resume."

"I wish you the best of luck with your job search. You are all set, I'll see you for your regular check-up. Enjoy your day," said Dr. Jones leaving the room.

*********************************

*That was the best news I have heard all day. I'm about fifteen minutes early for my physical-therapy appointment. I'll go sign in; maybe Dr. Thomas isn't with a patient.*

"I have a 4 o'clock appointment with Dr. Thomas," I told his receptionist.

"You lucked out. His 3 o'clock cancelled, so Dr. Thomas can see you now. Please follow me," said the nurse.

*Good, I'm ready to get my ass home. I'm hungry as hell. I guess I can call Rock and tell him to pick me up about 4:30 or 4:45.*

\*\*\*\*\*\*\*\*\*\*\*\*\*\*\*\*\*\*\*\*\*\*\*\*\*\*\*\*\*\*\*\*\*\*\*\*

"Rock, baby, I'll be ready at 4:30," I said through the phone

"Oh, I thought you wouldn't be ready until about 5 o'clock," said Rock, breathing heavy

"What's the matter? Why are you breathing so hard?" Asked Tracy.

"Oh, I just ran across the street to the car," said Rock.

I was getting angry. "I don't hear any cars going by or any noise. Where the fuck you at, Rock?"

"Damn, I said I was running to the car," said Rock, trying to stay calm.

"Whatever. I don't believe you. Just pick me up at 4:30." I hung up before Rock could say anything else.

*Damn! I almost got busted. I better get my ass up out of here before ol' girl wake up.*

# Chapter 6

## Tim

"Tim, come on and eat. You've been up there getting dressed for over a half hour. You sure you ain't going to meet your girlfriend?" asked Lisa, jokingly.

"Yeah, right," I scoffed, coming down the stairs.

"Well, you act like you going to meet your woman," Lisa said. "You're only meeting Rock, G, and Jason at the Back Door Bar. ...I know you haven't been out in a while..."

"Yeah, we haven't hung out for a few months—since the incident with Tracy," I said, unconsciously lowering my voice.

"You can catch up on things, find out what's been going on with everybody," said Lisa.

"You know you can go," I reminded her.

Now it was her turn to scoff. "Yeah, right."

"You can. My wife can go wherever I go," I claimed, grabbing Lisa around her waist.

"I don't think your boys will have a good time with me hanging around. They won't get to express their true selves if I'm standing there," said Lisa, folding her arms across her chest.

"I know." I kissed Lisa seductively on the lips for being so supportive, at the same time grabbing her ass—because I wanted to.

"Okay, don't start something you can't finish. I think you better eat your food, or you won't be making it to the Back Door Bar."

"I don't care about going to the bar; I think I'll have more fun right now with you," I said. I could feel myself rising just thinking about making love to Lisa.

It had been a few weeks since we had made love, and the feeling right now in my pants was starting to take control. I grabbed Lisa and pulled her close to me so that she could feel the bulge in my pants. I could feel her pussy pressing up against me. Her pussy was aching to be stroked.

I starting licking and sucking on Lisa's neck. "Damn, baby you smell so good" I put my hand under her shirt, and started rubbing her nipples. Lisa pulled her shirt off and grabbed my head and pulled it toward her nipple. I put it in my mouth and sucked on it like a baby's bottle. Lisa was already moaning and pulling at my pants. Finally she got the zipper down and pulled out my manhood. I knew it was just how she liked it—nice and hard. She started stroking my dick, putting it between her legs.

Lisa had on a skirt, but didn't have on any underwear—something I discovered when I reached under her skirt and put my finger in her soaking-wet pussy. I lifted Lisa up and put my dick inside her. Lisa threw her head back and starting sliding up and down on my dick like she was riding a horse. I wasn't about to let her ride alone; I joined her rhythm, and we both exploded, screaming in hot passionate love.

I put Lisa on top of the kitchen table and fell over on top of her, breathing hard.

"Damn, baby, that was good as hell. We got to do that more often. Fucking in the kitchen felt better than fucking in the bedroom," I panted, trying to catch my breath.

Lisa just lay there, legs shaking from her orgasm. She kept squeezing her legs together like she was trying to get her last drop of cum.

"Baby, baby, you all right?" I asked, getting up and trying to make my way to the bathroom with my pants still wrapped around my ankles.

Lisa propped herself up on her elbows and bust out laughing. "Baby, you look funny as hell. Pull your damn pants up, before you fall on your face."

"Shit, I'm trying to get to the bathroom so I can freshen up. See what you did."

"It's not my fault," laughed Lisa.

"Shit, I'm tired as hell now. I feel like taking a nap"

"See, I almost knocked your ass the fuck out," smirked Lisa, running around the kitchen table, pumping her hands in the air like she just won a fight.

"Oh, you got jokes, huh?" I asked, smiling

"Naw, I was overdue for some dick. You be putting me on punishment."

"Baby, I just be tired as hell when I get off work."

"I know, I know, my baby be working hard," said Lisa, mimicking me.

"I better get my ass out of here. If I lie down, I might not make it to the bar."

"Tell the fellas I said hi," said Lisa, walking into the bathroom.

"Damn, I got some spaghetti sauce on my shirt," How'd that happen? I didn't even have time to eat. Must've been from where Lisa was cooking the spaghetti.

"I'll grab you another shirt from upstairs," offered Lisa.

"Thanks, baby," I said gratefully.

"Throw the dirty shirt in the laundry room," she instructed.

"Okay. I'll call you when I'm on my way home."

"Have a good time and don't drink too much," hollered Lisa. I could tell she had her head in the closet.

"Grown-ass man, baby, grown-ass man," I laughed, hitting myself In the chest.

"Okay, grown-ass man," she said, sauntering downstairs with my clean shirt in hand, "just don't come in here throwing up. Talking about, 'Ooo, baby I don't feel good... I think I drank too much!'" said Lisa, mimicking me again.

"You got jokes, I see." I smiled again, taking the shirt from her and slipping it on.

"You know I'm telling the truth," Lisa laughed, solicitously helping me do the buttons.

"Thanks, baby. ...Baby, your ass is getting big, and I mean literally your back side!" said Tim, slapping her booty as she was walking away.

"I know. I need to start exercising again" said Lisa.

"Shit, you don't need to exercise. It looks good to me." I slapped it again, for emphasis.

"Whatever, it's probably them vitamins I've been taking," said Lisa.

"Them some good-ass vitamins!"

"Get your ass on to the bar," laughed Lisa.

I obeyed and took my ass on out of there.

\*\*\*\*\*\*\*\*\*\*\*\*\*\*\*\*\*\*\*\*\*\*\*\*\*\*\*\*\*\*\*\*\*\*\*\*

Did Tim notice anything? I hadn't been feeling good lately. I didn't want to jump to conclusions, but I knew the signs, and they were all there.

*I hope and pray I'm not pregnant. Tim is always saying he's not ready. Shit, when is the right time?*

*If I am pregnant, I definitely didn't plan this shit. I'm the one who will be walking around with a big-ass belly. But, then again, we're not getting younger, and my* mother is always bugging me about a grandchild.

I'm going to go out and buy one of those over the counter pregnancy tests.

# Chapter 7

**Tina**

*My business in New York didn't take as long as I thought it would. But, damn, it feels good to be home.*

*I still can't believe Mark ended up on the same flight to New York. I really enjoyed dinner with him the other night. The conversation was as if nothing ever happened. I wish him the best of luck with his modeling career. I better check on Tracy, see what she's been up to.*

# Chapter 8

**Tracy**

*R*ing, ring, rinnngggg

"Hello," I murmured, coming out of a deep sleep.

"Wake your ass up!" a voice said—I recognized it as Tina's. "It's almost 6 o'clock in the evening. Are you pregnant or something?"

"What did you say?" I asked, coming fully awake. *Could Tina know?*

"You heard me. Why you always sleeping throughout the day? Lately, every time I call your ass, you're sleeping or taking a nap," said Tina.

*Dr. Jones had told me I was pregnant during my check-up after the incident with Chris. I didn't know what I planned to do, that's why I hadn't told anyone, including Rock. I was scared because, when I counted back, the baby I was carrying could possibly be Mr. Ward's. I didn't' even want to think about that; the thought of carrying his baby made me cringe.*

*I knew I had to make a decision; I didn't' want to wait too long. I had so many thoughts running through my head. Should I tell Rock? Or just take care of it and keep my dark secret to myself? Either way, I had to make a decision, and fast, because I was getting close to the deadline if I wanted to terminate the pregnancy. I was leaning more toward Rock being the father because of the time frame. The only way to find out for sure would be to get Rock to take a blood test, and I knew he would start asking a thousand questions about why I wanted him to take the test.*

"Hello; I know you hear me," Tina shouted through the phone.

"I heard your ass; damn, I ain't deaf," I said, still distracted, still wondering what I should do.

*Should I tell Tina? She's like the sister I never had. Fuck it, I need to get this off my chest and tell somebody. Who better than Tina?*

"I'm pregnant. Now, I said it." I waited for a response from Tina.

No sound from the other end. Just silence.

"Did you hear what I said?"

"I heard you. I'm just speechless." said Tina.

"I've never known you to be speechless, Tina."

"Oookayyy...I'm trying to absorb this new found information from my BFF, so what are you going to do? Who's the daddy? Because I know you told me you fucked your old boss" blurted Tina. She sounded as if she were still in shock.

"Damn, you don't forget shit," I said.

"Your curious ass in trouble for real," said Tina.

"Fuck you, Tina." I cried, getting emotional

# Chapter 9

### Tina

I wasn't trying to get Tracy upset or emotional. I didn't mean to make her weep. But I had to tell her.

"I'm sorry, but that shit you did in the dark has caught up with your ass."

"I'm not having it," said Tracy before I could get another word in.

"'It'...damn, you are carrying a *baby*, not an *it*," I said.

"This is fucked up. You have to go with me, I can't do this alone." Pleaded Tracy.

"You know I'll support you, whatever decision you make, but please make sure this is what you want to do. Once it's done, you can't take it back. I just want you to be sure this is the right decision"

"I know this is the best decision for everyone. I'm going to call and make an appointment for an abortion,"

"Are you going to be all right?" I asked. *I could tell Tracy was probably about to start crying. She always gets emotional and cries.*

"Yeah, I'm going to get up and make me some tea. Maybe that will make me feel better. I have to see how I'm going to do this shit without Rock knowing."

"Just tell him Dr. Jones wants to run some more tests on you."

"Yeah, I'll tell him that. I'll let you know the date and time, so you can plan your day," said Tracy.

"Okay. I'll stop by later. I brought you back a cute outfit from New York."

*I hoped the news would cheer Tracy up.*

"Thank you. I was hoping you didn't forget about your sister." Tracy was delighted.

"Okay, you can stop smiling."

"How did you know I was smiling?"

"I can tell from your voice. Happy I could cheer you up. I'll see you later."

"Okay," said Tracy hanging up the phone.

*******************************

*Damn, my girl is pregnant! I always knew something like this would happen or worse. I told her ass to stop being so fucking curious about her boss. Now, she has to deal with this shit. She must decide if having an abortion is the solution to her problem. She's married to Rock, and I know this nigga will go the fuck off if he finds out it's not his.*

*To this day, no one knows that he killed Chris. I still can see him standing in the back of the crowd at the courthouse. He didn't even notice me looking right at him. At first I thought he saw me, but he turned around and walked out the door as if nothing happened.*

*I wanted to mention it to Attorney Patton, but I decided against it. Knowing what Tracy had been through, I couldn't do it. This is something I guess I will have to take to my grave. I hate thinking about it; no matter what a person has done, it's not up to us to take our own justice. Chris didn't deserve to die. Rock should have left it in God's hands.*

*"I wanted to go to confession, hoping it would make me feel better about my decision. But I chickened out. I know the priest would have told me to tell the police what I knew, and I can't do that. I don't*

*know how much longer I can keep this secret to myself. I might have to tell..."*

# Chapter 10

## Jason – Back Door Bar

"What up, dog? Damn, you look like you been putting on some weight," Jason blurted out when he saw Rock

"I know, I gained, like, twenty pounds, messing around with Tracy ass. Sitting up eating ice cream and cake late at night, then taking my ass to sleep. I've been hitting the gym, trying to work this shit off." said Rock, rubbing his belly.

"You'll be straight once we start up the league next month. Running your ass up and down the court will definitely make you lose weight. The pounds will start to drop off before you know it," Said Jason.

"Damn, Jason, I can't believe you gone start back hooping with us, that's straight. I know we can use somebody who got skills on the court, because we got some sorry ass nigga's right now. " Said Rock

"Y'all still got that bald-head nigga playing with y'all they call Dark Skin?" Asked Jason

"Yeah, that nigga is weak as hell, but he think he's the shit. Everybody on the team think he's a switch hitter" laughed Rock

"All hell naw" Said Jason, frowning up at the thought of Dark Skin

"I don't even want to picture that shit in my head. Let's talk about something else. How's my girl Tracy doing? Asked Jason.

"She's coming along alright. She has physical therapy once a week. You know I took a leave of absence to take care of Tracy? She tried to tell me she would be all right with a visiting nurse, but I know I would not have gotten any work done. I would have been calling every hour checking up on her. She really had me worried after the incident," Rock confessed.

"I know she did, because your ass up and married her right in her hospital bed. You couldn't even wait until she was discharged from the hospital. I was, like, 'Damn, ol' boy is serious!'—but I can't blame you, man; I would have done the same thing. That's why I wasn't trying to wait. I was going to marry Monica, but the unfortunate happened. As I always say, tomorrow isn't promised. That's good to hear Tracy is doing good"

"Yeah, she straight; she got a clean bill of health to go back to work."

"I know you were happy to hear that" Smiled Rock, leaning back in his chair.

"Hell yeah. Truthfully, I was getting tired of being at home. Nigga need a break every now and then," laughed Rock. He changed the subject: "Where the fuck are Tim and G?" he wondered, looking around the bar.

"G's ass is probably stuck at Shake That Ass," Laughed Jason.

"What? Hell naw, that nigga caught up in the tittie bar now?" Asked Rock.

"Hell yeah. Some broad named Nicky got that nigga hooked. He's in denial, but I see all the signs. Been there, done that. I told the nigga to be careful."

"Damn, he done got sprung on the pussy!" Rock couldn't stop laughing.

"Look who's coming through the door," Jason pointed.

"Tim and G. Damn, did them niggas go to the tittie bar together?" Rock started laughing at the thought of Tim in a tittie bar. He knew Lisa didn't play that tittie bar shit.

"What up, my niggas?" greeted Tim, giving Jason and Rock dap, and a brotherly hug.

"*You*, mannn..." laughed Rock, giving in to his humor again.

"Damn, G, please tell me you wasn't at the tittie bar." Said Jason.

"Man don't even go there. Don't worry about where I was at. I'm here now; just bring on the drinks. Nigga ready to get his drink on," smiled G.

"G, you a tittie-bar man now?" asked Tim

"Man, don't listen to Jason," said G.

"Call me the next time you go," said Rock, looking serious.

"Shitttt, man, Tracy ain't gone cuss my ass out for taking her husband to the tittie bar," said G, giving Jason dap.

"I know that's right," Tim joined in.

"Wait a minute, nigga," Rock teased Tim. "Why you so late? Did Lisa put the smack down on you, too?"

"Yeah, she put the smack down on me, all right, if you know what I mean," smiled Tim

"Aw, shit, what happened? Do tell nigga, do tell," said G.

"I don't kiss and tell. Remember, man, that's my wife we're talking about," said Tim.

"Aw...don't be getting all sensitive on a nigga; I was just playing, man" said G.

"I know, man," said Tim. "Just bring on the drinks. It's been a minute since we all got together. We need to catch up on things. I just know I'm ready to hoop."

"Yeah, that's what I'm talking about," said G, acting like he was dribbling an imaginary ball and shooting it.

# Chapter 11

## Back Door Bar

A beautiful black woman stood at the corner of the bar, watching Rock, Jason, Tim, and G.

She pointed at the quartet and asked the bartender who each of them was. She knew Rock; they had just been together earlier in the day. She needed to know who the other three gentlemen were. She was putting her plan into place, and she had to make sure she put the right individuals in their prospective places if her plan was going to be executed smoothly.

# Chapter 12

### Tracy

*I*'m glad Rock got out of the house. This gives me time to think about what I'm going to do about the baby. One side of me is saying keep the baby, but I'm not 100% sure it's Rock's. That's why I need a blood sample from him. This is killing me; I don't know what to do.

The doorbell rang.

*I hope that's Tina. I know she'll help me come up with what's best for everyone.*

"Hey, baby girl," Said Tina as she hugged Tracy and handed her some bags.

"You definitely know how to cheer a sista up," Said Tracy, digging around in the bags.

"Dr. Baker is in the house...." laughed Tina looking at Tracy digging in the bags like a little kid in a candy store.

Tracy's mood changed abruptly. "Damn, this is fucked up. I don't know what to do," Admitted Tracy.

"Well, weigh the pros and cons against each other," said Tina, "and try to come up with a plan."

"The only option I can see is to have an abortion."

"Have you really thought about this? Maybe you should tell Rock and see his reaction."

"Oh, hell naw. I already know what that nigga will say. "He believes in family.""

"Well, whatever you decide to do I got your back." Tina gave Tracy a sisterly hug.

"I know. You are the one person I can depend on."

"Okay, enough with the sad stuff. Open your bags. I want to see your reaction," smiled Tina sitting back on the couch.

"I already know you hooked a sista up. Did you meet any fine brothers while you were in New York?"

"You will never guess who was on the same flight as me and sitting right next to me. It fucked me up; I couldn't believe it."

"You know I hate guessing; just tell me," Said Tracy, eager with anticipation.

"Mark" said Tina, waiting to see Tracy's reaction.

"Hell nawww......." Screamed Tracy, laughing

"That shit ain't funny," laughed Tina.

"Yes, it is! I wish I could have seen your face when he walked up and sat next to your ass. You probably wanted to shit brick"

"You could have bought me for a fucking penny. I couldn't believe it, either, when I saw him. I was hoping he hadn't seen me. Him coming and sitting down next to me was the last thing I expected. I could have just jumped up and walked off the plane and caught another flight. But, believe it or not, we ended up having a decent conversation over dinner, almost like old times, minus the relationship."

"Shut the fuck up—no, you didn't!"

"Yes we did."

"You and Mark are friends now?"

"I didn't say we were friends; I'm just saying I have to let bygones, be bygones and move on with my life. I know Mark and Chris did some fucked-up shit to me, but I'm trying to move on from that. I have better things to worry about, like my business for one."

"Hey, how's that coming along?"

"Good, I should have my first shipment delivered in one month. I can't wait."

"Are you hiring?."

"You're funny; you know that, right?"

"I'm serious as hell, Shit, I need a fucking job."

"You know I got your back. I trust you with my life, so you know I would trust you with my company,"

"All....I feel special" said Tracy

*Tina changed the subject back to the original topic of conversation.*

"I have to say, Mark was looking good as hell as usual. It seemed like every woman on the plane was trying to hit on him. Little did they know, brother man wanted the same thing they did: some good dick."

*They both started laughing and giving each other high fives.*

"Now *that's* some funny shit" I declared Tracy, laughing.

"Where's your hubby?"

"At the Back Door bar. He's meeting Jason, Tim, and G."

"Fella's night out, huh?"

"Yeah, he needed to get out of the house. I know I probably have been driving him crazy."

"That's what wives are for, didn't you know," laughed Tina.

"All I know is that I have been horny as hell lately," admitted Tracy.

"That's the baby and your hormones," smiled Tina.

"No, that's from not having sex in weeks. Sista was long overdue. My poonanny was screaming for some dick."

"That's a little TMI."

"You're the sister I never had; I can tell you anything."

"I hope so, because I have something to tell you, too," Tina said teasingly.

"What?" Asked Tracy, eager with anticipation.

"Damn you been locked up in the house too long," laughed Tina.

"Come on, come on. Spill the hot gossip!"

"I've met someone," said Tina. She eyed Tracy sideways, looking for some type of reaction.

"Oohhh, what's his name and occupation? Wait a minute—what happened to Attorney James Patton?."

"We're friends, but I'm not feeling him in a physical way. He's fine as hell, a sweetheart; we have fun when we're together, but the physical attraction is not there. He's like my homey or just someone

I can kick it with. He understood where I was coming from."

"So, in other words, you don't want to strip butt-ass naked and fuck the shit out of him?" Laughed Tracy

"Yep, that's right. We are strictly hanging buddies, not fuck buddies"

"Damn Tina, that's fucked up. But I understand what you're saying; it's like that sometimes."

"I tried, but I wasn't feeling him. There was no emotion or passion when we were together. I told him my feelings on our relationship, and he says he understands, as long as we can still hang out together."

"Now that's what I call a real nigga. You don't want to fuck him, and he understands your feelings and still wants to continue to be your friend. Now let's get back to this new guy."

"Well...he's a doctor," smiled Tina, blushing.

"Where did you meet this doctor?" Asked Tracy, wanting to know more.

"Remember when you were in the hospital? He came in your room a few times when I was there. We exchanged little flirtatious remarks to each other. The more I flirted, the more I started to get attracted to him. Finally, he asked me out."

"And where did you go? And did you fuck him?" Tracy was pressing for more information.

"Damn, girl, I'm not a ho'. No we did not fuck on the first date, and he cooked dinner for me, if you must know."

"Dang, he's a doctor, and he can cook."

"Yep. I just feel so good when I'm around him. The chemistry is definitely there. Oh, by the way, I didn't mention that he's fine as hell, with a tight-ass body" smiled Tina

"Hmmm...what's this doctor's name?"

"Before I tell you his name, I wanted to let you know that he's not a brother," said Tina, once again trying to gauge Tracy's reaction.

"Ooohh, you go, girl. I ain't mad at you, because my Physical Therapist is white and is fine as hell for a white boy. I can't stop smiling whenever I'm around him, and he's always flirting with me."

"Heyyy...slow your ass down; remember you're married. Look at your left ring finger, Mrs. Johnson."

"I am a woman; I can still look and imagine."

"Imagine what?."

"You know: how it would be to fuck a white man."

"Damn, Tracy, didn't I warn you about this before with your old boss? Being curious as hell."

"I know; I know. I can have my fantasy without touching. So what is his nationality? Italian, Puerto Rican, Mexican?."

"He's white."

"Damn Tina. What's his name?"

"Dr. Richard Thomas."

I put my head down and felt like throwing up. I never expected Dr. Richard Thomas's name to come out of Tina's mouth. Out of all the doctors in the hospital, why did it have to be him?

I couldn't believe I was reacting like this. Did I have some feeling for this man or was it just a school-girl crush? Now all I could think about was if the two of them had had sex. I needed to know.

# Chapter 13

## Jason

I never thought I would be excited about a doctor's appointment. I couldn't wait until Monday. This was the only way I could get to see ol' girl. I remember her eyes were the first thing I saw when I woke up from surgery. She had hazel eyes and was leaning over me looking into my eyes with a flashlight, telling me that she was my doctor and that she came in to check on me. I felt kind of light headed, and my stomach felt upset from the anesthesia.

"Wait a minute, Mr. Davis, let me help you sit up. You may feel like you want to vomit; it's one of the side effects from the anesthesia. They should have given you a pill to take, but, under the circumstances, when emergency brought you in, there was no time for that," said Dr. Jones.

I felt very groggy, but I still could make out her face. She looked very young to be a doctor. Monica's death was still hanging over my head, and all I wanted to do at the moment was let out my pain of losing her. Before I knew it, tears were streaming down my face. Dr. Jones took a Kleenex and wiped my face. She was very gentle and kind. She seemed genuinely concerned about me.

"Are you all right? Can I get you anything?" she asked.

"I'm okay," I insisted, wiping my face with the back of my hand.

"If you need someone to talk to, I'm here to listen."

Her voice sounded so soothing, I thought I was dreaming. She sat on the side of my bed and held my hand. I didn't realize until I woke up the next day that I had fallen back to sleep while she was holding my hand. I buzzed for the nurse and asked her if anyone had called or come to see me. She informed me that a few people had come by asking about me.

"Mr. Davis, Dr. Jones requested that I contact her once you were awake. She came by earlier today to check on you, but you were still sleeping. The anesthesia does that sometimes. Can I get you anything?" asked the nurse.

"Maybe a piece of toast, or some crackers. I still feel kind of nauseated."

*****************************************

"Well, how's my patient this morning?" asked Dr. Jones

"A little nauseated, and sore from the surgery."

"You're a lucky young man. If that bullet had been any closer, it could have killed you."

"I need to talk to my brother."

"I'll have someone at the nurse's station contact your brother for you. What's his number?."

"(313) 550-1234."

"Okay, I'll give that to the nurse on my way out. I need to check your pressure and take a look at your incision."

"Ouch."

"Sorry, but I have to put a little pressure on it. We don't want any blood clots to form."

"Can I ask you a personal question?."

"Depends," smiled Dr. Jones.

"How old are you? You don't look old enough to be a doctor."

"Well, If you went straight through college, and medical school without any interruptions, you would still be young—but old enough to be a doctor."

"Twenty-six?" I was trying to guess her age

"Thanks for the compliment, but no. Don't you know you're never supposed to ask a woman her age?" laughed Dr. Jones.

"Sorry."

"You don't have to apologize. I'm asked that question quite often."

"Thanks for understanding. So Doc, how am I doing?."

"Everything looks good; you'll be here probably a few weeks. We want to make sure no infection sets in. I'll come back and check on you before I go home for the day."

\*\*\*\*\*\*\*\*\*\*\*\*\*\*\*\*\*\*\*\*\*\*\*\*\*\*\*\*\*\*\*\*\*\*\*\*\*\*\*\*\*

Over the course of those few weeks, I got to know Dr. Jones well. She was truly genuine, a nice person all around, and, to top it off she was a sister. She definitely had it going on, and she took my mind off thinking about Monica. I missed Monica, but I had to move on with my life.

I don't know why, but I couldn't get Dr. Jones off my mind. One day when she came to check on me, I kind of played around during our conversation and told her that her boyfriend better watch out I might steal her from him. She said that she didn't have a boyfriend and that she wasn't married.

I found out that she had a ten-year year-old daughter. Nurse Racquel, who I think had a crush on me, didn't hesitate to give me whatever information I asked for about Dr. Jones. From our conversations, ol' girl was hating on Dr. Jones. She was jealous as hell. She didn't have nothing nice to say about her. She stated that Dr. Jones never talked about her daughter's father.

Nurse Racquel made a point of being assigned to my room. She would come by every day and lean over me, putting her breast all over my chest or in my face. She should have caught the hint that I wasn't the least interested in her. I tried to be nice, letting her know that I had just lost my fiancée and wasn't trying to get into a relationship right now. That didn't faze her; she insisted that we could be friends and just hang out. She even put her number in my cell phone. Racquel had a tight-ass body, but she was too damn ghetto. I wonder how she passed nursing school. I was nice to her as long as she was giving me the information I wanted. I planned on using that information in the future to get a date with Dr. Jones.

\*\*\*\*\*\*\*\*\*\*\*\*\*\*\*\*\*\*\*\*\*\*\*\*\*\*\*\*\*\*\*\*\*\*\*\*\*\*\*\*

"I have a 12:30 appointment with Dr. Jones," Said Jason, coming out of his day dream state.

"Okay Mr. Davis, you can have a seat; someone will be calling you shortly," said the receptionist.

*I sat there wondering how I would go about asking Dr. Jones for a date. I'm scared I will be shot down. She's probably one of those doctors who don't date their patients. I know I'm from the streets, but I can be a gentleman when I want to. Maybe I should send her some flowers first. Shit, I'm acting like I've never asked someone out.*

"Mr. Davis, you can come back now," said Racquel smiling

*Damn, I must be cursed. How the hell did Racquel end up here at my appointment? I'm beginning to think she's stalking me now.*

"You look surprised; I know you didn't expect to see me," said Racquel, that same smile plastered to her face.

"Yeah, you definitely surprised me."

"Aren't you happy to see me? I see you haven't used my number," Racquel said, with an air of reproach.

"I'm sorry, but I lost my phone and had to buy a new one," I lied, trying not to show how I really felt.

*Why the fuck did I have to run into her?*

"Well I'll give you my number before you leave today," said Racquel, undaunted.

"Okay," I shrugged, walking past her without looking back.

"So, how's my patient?" greeted Dr. Jones coming into the room, and closing the door.

"I'm doing okay. I'm going to get straight to the point, Dr. Jones."

*She looked kind of shocked at my outburst.*

"Uh, what point is that, Jason?"

"Can I take you out to dinner?"

"I have a rule: I don't date my patients."

"I can respect that," I said, trying to think of something else quick. Damn....I hope I haven't fucked up by asking her out.

# Chapter 14

## Dr. Jones

I was attracted to Jason as well, but I didn't let on to anyone. I always was attracted to tall, strong, athletic men with a little thug in them. Jason definitely fit the part. I had made a promise to myself years ago that I would never date that type of man again. My relationship with my daughter's father tore a hole in my heart that I couldn't seem to mend.

But something about Jason drew me to him; I didn't know if it was the night that I sat there and held his hand while tears streamed down his face or if it was a physical attraction. So far, I had kept our relationship professional—strictly doctor and patient—but the deep feelings for him that I was trying to keep buried were slowly starting to creep out. I was just as excited about his appointment as he was. I was looking forward to seeing him; I found myself putting on perfume the day of his appointment. I knew I didn't want my feelings to get in the way of my career as a doctor, and I had my daughter to think about as well. I was still feeling guilty, because I had never told my daughter who her father was. She was ten years old now, and was starting to ask questions about him. Sooner or later I would have to tell her.

*****************************************

"Dr. Jones, calling Dr. Jones" said Jason, bringing me out of my trance. Are you all right?"

"I'm sorry; I just drifted off."

"What were you so deep in thought about? Going on a date with me I hope." Smiled Jason, hoping to lighten up the situation.

"Jason, I'm thrilled about your invitation, but I can't date my patients."

"Okay. As of today, Jason Davis is no longer your patient. I'm changing doctors"

"I don't know if this is right, Jason."

"Just go on one date with me. I promise, if you don't enjoy my company, then I will understand if you don't want to go out with me anymore."

*He gave Dr. Jones this sad puppy-dog look.*

"Okay: one date. You better not tell anyone, Jason—I'm not playing."

"Okay, okay, look at you trying to sound all hard."

"Hey, don't let this doctor's coat fool you. I'm from the ghetto."

"Now, who would have thought? Can we make it for this Friday night, at 7:00?."

"Let's make it a late date: 8:30; my shift ends at 7:00, and I like to freshen up before I go on a date."

*Dr. Jones folded her arms across her chest smiling at Jason.*

"It's a date, then. I'll see you on Friday." Said Jason

"I'll leave you a text message with my number and home address. Now that we've settled that, can I finish your check-up?"

"Just tell me where you want me, doc." Said Jason, unbuttoning his shirt. *Racquel stood outside the door listening to their whole entire conversation.*

# Chapter 15

## Tina

*D*amn, *Tracy was acting funny as hell after I told her who I was seeing. I thought she would be cool with me dating a Caucasian man; at least, from our conversation, that's what I felt. Oh, well, she'll get over it. I'm a grown-ass woman. Maybe it's her hormones acting up. I'm definitely going to talk to her about it. I'm ready to just relax in front of the tv and watch a good movie.*

Then I heard the chimes.

*Who the fuck is ringing my doorbell? I wasn't expecting anybody.*

"Who is it?"

"Alexis."

I peered through the eyehole. *What the fuck is she doing at my door?*

*Let me pull myself together. I have no idea why she's here. Maybe she wants to find out what happened between me and Chris. —I hate to bust your bubble, honey, but your brother was down-low.*

"What brings you here today?" I asked, opening the door for Alexis.

"I was in the neighborhood," Alexis explained, "and I remembered you gave me your address at the funeral. I thought I'd stop by to see how you were doing."

"Oh, I'm doing okay. Keeping myself busy," I said, feeling uncomfortable.

*Alexis seemed to sense my discomfort.* "I'm sorry; I should have called," she said.

"That's okay; come on in." I tried to be cordial.

"I'm glad I got to meet you. You have to excuse my mother and father. I know they were not the friendliest people. They are stuck in their old traditional ways. They always thought Chris should have married his high-school sweetheart. After we were informed of his death, they kept blaming you. I told them that what happened wasn't your fault," said Alexis

Before I knew it, I blurted out.

"Did you know your brother was gay?" I needed to know if his family knew, since they were blaming me for his death.

"Yeah, I knew. But my parents and my little brother didn't know until his death," said Alexis.

"He told you"? I was shocked that she knew.

"No, he didn't come right out and tell me. I always knew," said Alexis, looking steadily at me.

"So, you knew your brother liked men?" I was still shocked.

"I knew when we were kids that Chris liked boys. He would always want to play hide and seek. One of the neighbor's sons was gay, and he didn't' hide it. He let all the kids know. Chris was about 12, then. I would look at the way Chris paid so much attention to our neighbor's son whenever he came around. I never approached Chris and asked him, I just knew deep down. I didn't want to judge my brother; no matter what he preferred, I still loved him. So I never said anything about it to him. That's why, when I heard what happened, I wasn't shocked to find out about Mark"

"Did Mark call your parents?" I had to ask; I wanted to know everything.

"Yes. My parents accused him of making Chris gay. I chose not to say anything; they were grieving over the loss of my brother."

"I'm so sorry."

"I'm okay now," said Alexis.

"Can I get you anything to eat or drink? I forgot my manners."

"Do you have any wine?" asked Alexis.

"Red or white?"

"White," said Alexis

*************************************

*I woke up in bed, butt naked and very drowsy.*

*Damn, I can't remember what happened last night. The last thing I remember was me and Alexis laughing and drinking glasses of wine. I recall Alexis telling me that I looked tense; she walked over and started giving me a massage. Alexis was rubbing and massaging my shoulders, and up and around my neck. After that, everything is a blank.*

*What was really puzzling to me was the fact that I was lying in my bed, naked and had no recollection of how I got this way.*

*Deep down, I knew what happened, but I didn't want to admit it. The way I felt between my legs, I knew what transpired in my bedroom.*

*I was sitting there asking myself how the hell I let this happen. I got up and* decided to take a shower to try and clear my head. I wanted so badly to remember what happened last night.

After my shower, I went downstairs. There on my living room table were three empty bottles of wine. Damn, I can't believe we drank three bottles of wine! How in the hell did I let this happen?

As I started to clean up, I found a note on the table. The minute I started reading it, sweat broke out on my forehead and my hands started shaking. The note slipped out of my hand and dropped to the floor.

The last words on the note were all in caps:

I GOT YOU ON VIDEO TAPE. NOW YOU KNOW HOW MY BROTHER FELT. NOW LOOK WHO'S STUCK IN THE DARK!!!!

# Chapter 16

**Lisa**

"Baby," I asked Tim, "did you have a good time at the bar last night?."

"Yeah, I needed that. Just me and the fellas kicking back, talking sports and shit."

"I know, you were starting to get on my nerves."

I got the rise out of him that I was hoping for.

"What!?" said Tim.

His reaction amused me. "I was just playing, baby. I know you miss hanging out with your boys." Delicately, I changed the subject. "...I need to talk to you about something important, Tim."

"You're scaring me now, you look too serious."

"It is serious. I'm scared myself because I don't know how you are going to react."

"React to what?."

"I'm pregnant."

Tim sat there in silence. He started rubbing his bald-head. I started to get worried. I wanted to yell, "Say something—*do* something, will you?" But I kept quiet and waited for him to stop rubbing his head and look at me.

When he finally looked up, he had the biggest smile spread across his face. It made me grin, too.

"So, say something, baby!" I shouted.

"Baby, you have just made me the happiest man in the world."

"But, I thought you wasn't ready for children now."

"I know I've said that in the past, but we're not getting any younger. I want to be able to play basketball and baseball with my son without having to complain about being tired or too old."

"Baby, you have made me so happy. I didn't know how to tell you, but I knew it had to be said sooner or later."

"How far along are you?."

"I don't know for sure, but I think about six weeks."

"Well, we need to make a doctor's appointment so we can find out officially when my son will be born."

"Hey, who says it's going to be a boy?"

"I have strong genes. I know I ain't making nothing but boys," he asserted, grabbing hold of me, kissing me passionately.

"Okay, you know what happened the other day when you started that shit."

"I can handle that."

"Whatever."

*I feel so relieved. I really didn't want to terminate the pregnancy. We're not getting any younger, and I don't want to wait too long to have a baby. After all, both of our careers are steady now. I'll be teaching online college courses part-time. My first love is teaching elementary-school children. Being around kids all day at work, I used to daydream about the baby. Who it would look like—would it have Tim's nose or my eyes? Would it be a girl or boy? What would we name the baby?*

*A big weight has been lifted off my shoulders, I can relax now. I'm definitely looking forward to having our baby.*

# Chapter 17

**Tracy**

*I* can't believe my reaction. I know Tina is probably tripping on me. Why am I letting this get to me? Do I really have feelings for this man I've never even been intimate with? I think I'm just infatuated with the fact that a white man is paying me some attention—and a cute one at that.

"Tracy, I'm going to the store. Do you need anything?" asked Rock, pulling me out of my trance.

"I have a taste for some cookies and ice cream."

"Lately you been eating a lot of sweets; are you pregnant?."

"No, why do you ask?" I looked at Rock. *He couldn't possibly know—could he?*

"Just wondering why you've been eating like you can't get enough."

"Probably that new medication the doctor has put me on."

"Okay, I'll pick up the cookies and ice-cream. Do you want me to cook something to eat or do you want to eat out. We haven't been out to dinner in a while."

"That sounds good. Let's make a night of it. Let's go to Chili's or maybe that new steak house they just opened in Taylor on Telegraph Road," I suggested.

"Okay, get dressed, and we can leave as soon as I get back."

*Maybe getting out of the house is just what I need—to be around other people. Maybe that's why I've been having these feelings for Dr. Thomas. Lately going to my doctor's appointments are the only times I really got out.*

*My other problem needs to be addressed—and soon. God, please give me a sign to do the right thing. Right now, the only option I see is to get an abortion, and there's no way in hell I can tell Rock.*

# Chapter 18

### Rock

"Baby, this is just what we needed. A break away from the house," Tracy said.

*I was happy I could please her.*

"I already know what I'm going to order," Said Rock , setting his menu aside.

"Your usual, baby back ribs."

"Yep, you know your man. And you're going to order the Chicken crispers, your favorite. —Hey, the game's on; can we switch seats?."

"I can't believe you want to switch seats. You always want to be facing the door."

"I know, but I can't see the tv from my seat. Besides, you don't like to watch hockey."

"You're right about that."

"May I take your order?" asked the waitress as she approached our table.

*As we were giving the waitress our food order, a young lady walked in with a gentleman. I almost choked on my beer.*

"Baby, are you all right?" asked Tracy.

"Yeah," *I lied.* "When I swallowed, it went down the wrong pipe. Excuse me; I need to go to the bathroom."

"You okay, baby?" asked Tracy again.

"Yeah, I just need to go to the bathroom and freshen up. I kind of spilled beer on myself."

*I was sweating bullets, wondering if I should tell Tracy I wasn't feeling good or if I should just stay and hope the woman didn't see me. As I was making my way back to the table, she was walking right in my direction. She looked up and saw me, and a smirk came across her face.*

*I hurried to my seat, hoping the worried look on my face wasn't too visible. I was praying that she wouldn't say anything to me in front of Tracy, but I already knew from the look on her face that she definitely going to let it be known that she knew me.*

*She walked right up to the table, bent over, whispered in my ear, and kept walking.*

*From the look on Tracy's face, I already knew pure hell was about to break loose.*

# Chapter 19

## Jason

*L*ook at me acting like I'm going on my first date and shit. This is different, she's special. There's something about her that seems to bring out the best in me. When I'm in her presence, I want to act like a gentleman. She definitely brings out the good in me. I can see the two of us in a long-term relationship.

Mmm, mmm— Damn! I look good.

I better get going, I don't know how traffic is going to be. I hope she enjoys where we're going tonight. I have something special planned after we leave the restaurant. Hopefully she won't brush me off too quick.

Damn, this is a nice as neighborhood. Okay, my breath smells good. Can't be all up in nobody face with file-ass breath.

I rang the doorbell, and the sound made me jump.

Whew, I'm nervous as hell! Jason, straighten the fuck up! Damn, I'm acting like I've never been on a date.

# Chapter 20

### Dr. Jones

I opened the door, and there he was, smiling from ear to ear.

"Hey, miss lady, ready to go?"

*I couldn't help but smile ol' boy was looking good as hell.*

*Damn, I hope I don't get myself in trouble with this man. I know I should have said no, but my heart told me to give him a chance.*

On the ride to the restaurant, the conversation was lively and easy—we talked with one another as if we'd known each other for years. We had so much in common. He actually watched The Housewives of Atlanta. I told him that was one of my favorite shows. I didn't think men watched that show. He said the ghetto-ness of the show is what kept his attention. He said the show was funny as hell.

Before we knew it, we were pulling up to valet parking in front of an exclusive five-star hotel. I knew Grand Martino's was one of the most expensive hotels in Michigan, but I was wondering why we were there.

*Just what does he have in mind, anyway?*

# Chapter 21

## Jason

"Before you jump to any conclusions," I rushed to reassure her, "inside the hotel there's this new restaurant that opened up about a month ago, with a live jazz band that plays every night. I was told that it's really nice. I wanted to bring you somewhere with a relaxing atmosphere; you deserve it," I said sincerely, looking at how beautiful she was.

"I'm sorry, I should have waited. I didn't even give you a chance to say anything. I guess my expression showed, huh?" asked Dr. Jones.

"That's okay; I plan on showing you the time of your life in one night. So hold on tight, doc," I smiled, taking her hand and leading her up to the hotel entrance.

**********************************

"Jason, everything about this place is so romantic and relaxing. I'm really enjoying myself," enthused Dr. Jones.

"Thank you, but the night is not over yet."

"Oh, and what else do you have planned?."

The jazz band was playing soft, mellow music. I kept watching how Dr. Jones would close her eyes and sway to the rhythm of each song. She was definitely in a relaxed mood.

After the last song played, the band leader announced that he had a special song that was being dedicated to Dr. Tamika Jones. Tamika looked at me. That smile was worth what it cost to get the band to play her song.

# Chapter 22

**Dr. Jones**

I didn't know if it was the wine or the soft, mellow music that had put me in this laid-back mood, but I was in it, up over my head.

The band started playing, and, when Jason asked me to dance, I didn't hesitate.

As our bodies intertwined on the dance floor, Jason glided me around as if we were the only people in the room. Soon, we were moving in a slow motion as if we were making love. I could feel his manhood rising. It felt so good against my body; I wanted to take Jason right there in the room.

He brought my head close to him and starting kissing me right there on the dance floor. We got so caught up in each other that one of the patrons hollered, "Get a room!."

That made us laugh. We walked off the dance floor holding hands. Once we sat down, we just kept staring at each other.

Without saying a word, we both got up. Jason left the money for the food and the waitress's tip on the table. He went directly to the front desk, paid for a room, and we walked, still hand in hand, toward the elevator. Jason was so caught up in Tamika, he didn't notice the young lady staring at him from across the room.

# Chapter 23

### Lisa

"Tim, I think we should invite everyone over for dinner and announce our special news to them."

"Hook it up, baby," Tim encouraged Lisa. "Let's make it a month from now; that'll give us time to plan it."

"Okay, that's sounds good. It'll give me time to put a menu together and see what kind of adult games we can play to make the night fun," I enthused, excited about putting together a dinner.

"Do you think we should send out written invitations?" asked Tim.

"Yeah, let's make it nice. Guests can come casual. We want everyone to feel relaxed and comfortable."

"Well, I'm about to take a shower and watch the game. I just feel like relaxing and drinking me some beer."

I could hear the water running as I did the dishes in the kitchen. "Baby, how's Jason handling his brother being locked up?" I hollered to Tim.

"I know he's worried," he yelled back, over the noise of the shower, "but he's trying to stay strong. He said he hates visiting him. It's hard looking at his brother locked up, knowing that he's in there for a while."

"He just needs to pray for his brother," I said in a loud voice. "There's a reason for everything, even though, we don't like it. Only God's knows why—" Tim appeared in the doorway, toweling himself off, and I lowered my voice to normal. It definitely should be a learning tool for Jason."

"Oh, he has certainly changed in that sense," Tim assured me, tying the towel around his waist, grabbing a beer from the refrigerator, and padding into the family room to turn on the tv. "He said he's done with the drug game. He's taken his little stash and invested it in some stock that seems to be doing so well that he doesn't have to work for a few years."

"Damn, what stock is that?" Asked Lisa following Tim into the family room.

"He didn't say, and I didn't ask," said Tim, propping his feet up, switching on the remote to the hockey game, and taking a swig of beer.

I stood there staring at my husband. He was so in tune with the tv he didn't even notice me standing there watching him.

I figured I knew what kind of stock Jason had invested in. *I can't believe my husband is so lame. My baby was too sheltered growing up. Jason's stock is in the drug game—that shit is hard to let go. I've seen it happen too many times to a number of people I grew up with. You either end up dead or in jail. That fast profit looks good to anybody. Shit, I even tried it myself, growing up in the ghetto. But the difference between me, and Jason was I got in and got out quickly. I got out of it what I needed and moved on with my life.*

Tim's full attention was still on the tv. I decided now was a good time to make an appointment with the OB/GYN.

****************************************

"Tim, wake up."

"I'm up," he insisted, jerking awake. "What time is it?" he asked, stretching.

"It's 2:25 in the morning; go get in bed. You know you have to get up for work in four hours. You must have been really tired. You fell asleep during the game."

"You better get you some sleep too; my son is probably tired," smiled Tim, rubbing my stomach.

"Okay; don't be surprised if it's a girl," I laughed, pulling Tim up off the couch.

"I'm going to get up for work earlier so I can make you breakfast before I go to work. You know you're eating for two now, and I need to make sure my baby is eating right. I know that school cafeteria food is nasty as hell."

"Damn, are you okay? We've been married how many years now? You have never offered to make me breakfast. If anything, you offer to take me to Denny's or Bob Evans. I better not complain and just enjoy it while it lasts."

"Come on, baby, let's go to bed," said Tim. He swept me off my feet and carried me to the bedroom.

"Night, baby," I whispered in his ear.

"Good night, baby," he mumbled, already drifting off to sleep.

# Chapter 24

**Tracy**

"Who the fuck was that broad, Rock? Are you fucking her? *Huh?*" I screamed.

I think everyone in the restaurant must have heard me. I didn't care, and I didn't even give Rock a chance to answer. Instead, I punched him dead in the face. He grabbed me and held me down so I couldn't hit him again.

Somebody had called the police. The cops came and escorted us outside. The officer gave each of us a warning before letting us go.

We rode home in silence. I knew why *I* was quiet; I figured Rock was busy trying to think of some excuse to give me about the bitch who'd whispered in his ear.

Finally, he spoke.

"Tracy, you didn't even give me a chance to say shit."

"I can't believe you sat there and let that ghetto broad whisper in your ear and didn't even try to say anything to her. Like, 'This is my wife sitting across from me" That's would have been nice. But, naw, your dumb ass just sat there like you wanted to hear what she had to tell you. I should have gone in the bathroom and whooped her ass. I can't believe this shit just happened. Rock, we're married; if you still want to go out there and slang your dick up in every pussy you see, then we shouldn't have gotten married!" I couldn't help crying.

"Tracy, I don't even know that broad; she was giving me a compliment."

"That's bullshit, Rock. You can't come up with a better one then that? You ain't that motherfucking fine. If a nigga would have come whispering in my ear, you would have hit the motherfucking roof, accusing me of fucking the nigga. Don't say shit to me until you come to me with the truth."

We rode the rest of the way in total silence.

As soon as we stepped in the house, I went and left a message on my doctor's voicemail to schedule an abortion. Rock helped to make up my mind; there was no way in hell I was going to be pregnant and worry about him fucking somebody else. Besides, I really didn't know who the father was. What happened tonight only made my decision easy. *Tomorrow I'll call Tina first thing in the morning and let her know what I've decided to do.*

# Chapter 25

**Dr. Tamika Jones**

"Close the door and take off your clothes," I told Jason urgently.

"No, I want you to undress me," he insisted, coming to stand before me.

*I got off the bed and started unbuttoning his shirt. Damn, his body looks so good. Even the scars on his chest. I took my finger and slowly traced each scar, and kissing each one along the way. I started unfastening his pants and, pulled his silk boxers down. I gasped at the size of his penis standing erect. Damn, can I handle this? I had to ask myself. I was scared, but hot and horny at the same time.*

I took that big thing in my hand, which seemed so small by comparison, and started stroking it. The friction of stroking his penis seemed to make it even bigger.

I knew I was doing a good job because, in no time at all, Jason started moaning how much he wanted to make love to me. *Well, now he's gonna have to wait for me.*

I pushed Jason back on the bed and straddled him. I started licking and kissing him from head to toe, even sucking each finger—pulling and sucking them like they were lollipops.

Precum was dripping from the head of his penis. I licked every drop of that, too. I put the tip of his penis in my mouth and started a slow sucking motion. His penis was so big that I could only suck the tip, but it was doing the job because Jason's moans got louder and louder. He started moving his body up and down to the rhythm of my sucking.

The pace was picking up; I knew where I wanted him to be, and that the time had come to get there. I sat on top of his penis and rode it like a cowgirl. His ecstatic moans filled my ears just as his penis filled my vagina.

I did some moaning of my own, throwing my head back and screaming, "Fuck me. Jason; *fuck me!*" My screams of pleasure out weighted the pain I was feeling from the size of his penis.

He turned me over and started fucking me doggy style. I spread my ass cheeks so he could penetrate me further and yelled for him to fuck me harder. Jason pounded away with his penis while slapping my ass—I was in heaven!

"Baby, don't stop; I'm coming; *I'm coming—*"

We exploded as one. Jason collapsed on top of my back. He was breathing so hard, I thought he was going to have a heart attack. *Good thing I'm a doctor.*

"Damn, baby, you trying to kill me?" groaned Jason weakly, trying to lift himself up.

"I'm sorry, baby, but it's been awhile," I laughed.

"I can tell. Damn, you wore a nigga out. I'm tired as hell. Come on, baby, let's take a shower and go to sleep."

He picked me up in his arms and carried me to the bathroom. He was so gentle. He took the bath sponge and lathered me up from head to toe. I just stood there under the shower, watching him in awe. I closed my eyes and let Jason take control of my mind, body, and soul. The circular motion of the bath sponge on my body was igniting another fire within me. I opened my eyes to find Jason bending down and lifting my leg up. He started licking and sucking the inner part of my thigh, while making his way up to my vagina. I couldn't hold back any longer, I grabbed his head and started pushing it into my vagina. I felt an explosion coming that I didn't want to miss. He had skills with his tongue I had never experienced. I released his head and started grabbing onto the shower walls. I started screaming his name, the powerful orgasm I was having was unbelievable. I collapsed from the sexual explosion I had just had. Jason thought I had fainted.

"Baby, baby are you alright"? said Jason picking me up

"Yes..." was all I could mumble, I was so drained from my orgasm.

"Are you sure? You scared the hell out of me"

"I'm okay, just lay down with me and hold me"

"What time do you have to go in to work tomorrow?" said Jason carrying me from the bathroom

"I'm off tomorrow," I said slyly, nuzzling Jason's neck.

"Aw, shit—it's on and popping," said Jason, turning around and carrying me back to the bed.

"What do you mean by 'on and popping'? This woke me up out of my sexual trance. You trying to wear my pussy out? —Oh, hell naw," I feigned reluctance.

"Damn, baby, such language coming from a doctor," Jason laughed

"Don't let the title fool you. I told you I'm from the 'hood." I couldn't help but laugh right along with Jason. I was really enjoying his company, and the love making was unbelievable. Was I dreaming?

"I'm about to take care of my baby," said Jason

"Oh, I'm your baby now?" I had to admit, I liked the sound of that. I hadn't felt this good with a man in years, not since I'd been with my daughter's father.

I decided to enjoy the moment while it lasted.

We took turns rubbing each other down again in the shower, then kissed and made love over and over again. We finally fell asleep in each other's arms.

I woke up more than once and just stared at Jason, wondering if he were like this all the time or whether this was just a front to impress me.

Only time would tell.

# Chapter 26

**Tina**

I sat there with the note lying on the floor at my feet. I was in a state of shock.

What the fuck did she mean by "NOW LOOK WHO'S STUCK IN THE DARK." Was she talking about my nudity or what?.

*I can't believe she fucking video-taped me—doing what? I need to know what the fuck happened to me. I may have to go to a hypnotist to find out. Maybe Alexis drugged me; she must have! There's no way in hell why I shouldn't be able to remember what happened. As much as I drink wine, I know it did not do this to me. What did I do to her to deserve this? I didn't make her brother do what he did to Tracy. I didn't pull the trigger on the gun that killed him. I know who did, but I'm taking that to my grave. I need to see if I can get an appointment today with a doctor. I need to get myself checked out. This is scary as hell.*

**********************************

"Ms Baker, all the test results came back negative for any sexual diseases. Is there anything else you wanted me to check before you leave?" asked the doctor.

"Can you refer me to a hypnotist?"

The doctor had a puzzled look on her face. "May I ask why?"

"Uh, I just have a few questions." *Why is this doctor being so fucking nosy?*

*I can't ask Richard, because he would be asking me the same question. I just need to find out what happened, and fast. I want to call Alexis, but I know I would go the fuck off as soon as she answered the phone. I'm going to get back at her ass. You can bet on that.*

"Dr. Simpson is located right here in the hospital. I'm sure he'll be glad to answer any questions you may have. You can tell him I referred you," said the doctor.

I thanked her and left.

*I wonder what Tracy is up to. I'm going to see if she wants to do lunch.*

**\*\*\*\*\*\*\*\*\*\*\*\*\*\*\*\*\*\*\*\*\*\*\*\*\*\*\*\*\*\*\*\*\***

"What's up, girl?" answered Tracy.

"You hungry?" I asked.

"Hell, yeah! You treating? You know I don't have a job," laughed Tracy through the phone

"Whatever. Your ass got money; you just holding on to it. Remember: we used to be roommates. Your ass was always putting up money for a rainy day, and I know you ain't changed that much."

"Chili's?" asked Tracy

"Yeah, my favorite place. I'll get you in about thirty-minutes. So be ready, with your slow ass," I laughed.

"See, you getting all smart and shit. I'm already dressed."

"Oh, my God, Tracy is dressed, and it's not even 1:00 p.m. Damn, what's wrong with you?"

"I'll tell you about it when you pick me up."

"What happened?" I was concerned.

"Just come on and pick me up."

I got off the phone and jumped on the lodge freeway, heading toward Tracy's house.

# Chapter 27

## Jason

Finally I get to meet her daughter, I hope she likes me. I been seeing Tamika now going on three weeks, and it seems like months. I can't get enough of her. We have so much in common. I can sit and talk to her about anything for hours at a time and not get bored or tired. I think I'm falling in love with her. I hope she got the roses I had delivered today. I sent a different-color rose in a beautiful crystal glass vase. Each rose expresses a different feeling I have for her.

I'm taking her with me to the dinner that Tim and Lisa invited me to. Tim said I could bring a date. This way everybody will get to meet her. They have been dogging me *out because I haven't let none of them niggas meet her yet. They didn't even believe me when I told them she was a doctor. I can't wait for them to meet her. I know them niggas gone be tripping.*

*I told her we should take her daughter to Dave and Buster's sometime; I think she will enjoy that. I had a little bouquet of flowers delivered for her too. I know Tamika's going to be surprised.*

\*\*\*\*\*\*\*\*\*\*\*\*\*\*\*\*\*\*\*\*\*\*\*\*\*\*\*\*\*\*\*\*\*\*\*\*\*\*\*

"Baby, the flowers are beautiful" cried Tamika through the phone.

"I'm glad you like them; each rose represent my feeling for you."

"That is so sweet, baby…"

"Did Sya get her flowers?"

"She hasn't made it in from school yet. Her bus should be pulling up any minute now," said Tamika.

I changed the subject. "Tamika, how come you don't like to talk about Sya's father?"

It had been bothering me that Tamika never mentioned Sya's father or whether he was still a part of the child's life. A real man would want to take care of his kid. I didn't hesitate letting Tamika know that I wanted children.

"Jason, I'm going to be honest with you. Sya's father doesn't know she exists."

"You didn't tell him you were pregnant with his child?" asked Jason.

"I know I should have, but I didn't want him to feel that I was holding him back from his career or going pro," said Tamika, getting emotional.

"Baby, I'm not trying to get you upset, but it's not fair. If it were me I would be mad as hell at you when I found out. Whoever her father is, he has missed out on a lot in her life."

"I know. I've thought about it, and it's time I told Sya and her father. First, I have to find out where he is. I lost touch with him after I found out I was pregnant. I was the one who broke it off with him."

"Well, I'm glad to hear you've had a change of heart. You are the sweetest, sexiest person I know, and I know you have a good heart."

"Thank you, baby." I could tell Tamika was smiling through the phone.

"I'm going to pull out of here in about an hour, so be ready, Miss lady."

"I'll see you when you get here," said Tamika.

"Bye, baby."

"Bye."

# Chapter 28

## Tamika

I smiled, thinking about Jason, after I hung up the phone.

*I think I should wait until Jason and I get back from his friends' dinner, before I tell Sya about her dad. I'm going to have to prepare myself for this—and for the thought of looking him in the face after all these years.*

# Chapter 29

## The Dinner Party

So much had happened over the last few weeks. Relationships were made and some were broken. Tracy went ahead with the abortion without Rock's knowledge. Tina was at her side through the whole procedure. They both cried. Tina decided to confide in Tracy about her encounter with Alexis—and Tracy wanted to go fuck Alexis up good. They both were curious now as to what had been video taped.

Everyone was excited about the dinner party. They hadn't been together at the same time in one room since the ordeal with Tracy that ended up in the hospital.

So meeting up for a good time over dinner and drinks was what everyone needed.

Tracy forgave Rock, but she still let him know she didn't appreciate the shit that went down.

Tina had invited Dr. Thomas to the dinner. He informed Tina that he would be running a little late, because he was covering for another doctor. Tina failed to mention to Tracy that she had invited him.

Tina and Tracy were acting like high-school girls on the phone, curious to see who Jason and G's dates were. They had heard that Jason was bringing a doctor. G's date was an unknown; he said he wanted to surprise them.

"Baby, is everything all set? They should be arriving any minute now," said Lisa, all excited. She had been counting the days to this moment, when she would get everyone together again. It would be like old times.

"Relax, boo, I got everything all set," said Tim, giving Lisa a kiss on the lips.

They were so happy lately. Maybe it was the excitement of knowing that a baby would be in the house. That was definitely going to be a change.

*Ding, dong, ding, dong.*

"Baby, get the door," said Lisa.

"What up, nigga?" asked G, giving Tim dap and a manly hug.

"You, mannn..." smiled Tim.

"Tim, this is Alexis," smiled G, looking at Tim for his approval.

"Welcome to our home, Alexis; you look familiar," said Tim, trying to figure out where he had seen Alexis.

"I'm Chris's sister. I saw you at his funeral," said Alexis.

"Right...I saw you, but I didn't know you were his sister," said Tim, frowning and looking at G.

"Yeah. I've heard so much about you," smiled Alexis.

"Really? And I haven't heard anything about you," said Tim, still looking at G.

"Well, we've only been seeing each other for about two weeks. I'm embarrassed to tell you where we met," said Alexis.

"We're all adults; do tell," said Tim, now wanting to know.

"Heyyyy...leave her alone. She's a guest," said Lisa, coming out of the kitchen.

"Thank you for rescuing me," said Alexis smiling.

"Let's go in the family room," said Tim. "We have snacks and beer, and the Wii's set up for all you sports fanatics. It's a fun game—me and Lisa are always playing it. Alexis do you want some wine?"

"That would be nice," said Alexis.

G and Alexis went into the family room and sat down. Tim and Lisa stayed in the kitchen, whispering about the fact that G was dating Chris's sister.

"Baby, I swear I didn't know until they walked through the door," said Tim. He knew Lisa didn't like surprises.

"How the hell did they end up together? What a coincidence," said Lisa.

"I know; that shit don't add up to me," said Tim.

*Ding, dong, ding, dong.*

"Hey, G, can you get the door? I'm helping my wife in the kitchen," hollered Tim.

"Yeah, man, I got it," said G, heading toward the door.

"What up, nigga?" hollered Jason.

"You dog," said G.

"G, I would like you to meet my beautiful baby, Dr. Tamika Jones," smiled Jason, watching G's expression.

G just stood there staring at Tamika. He couldn't believe she was standing in front of him. He hadn't seen her since college. Tamika's expression was just as numb as G's. Jason stood there looking at both of them, wondering what the fuck was going on.

# Chapter 30

## Tina

*I better check with Richard again to see what time he's leaving work. He told me he had taken a change of clothes to work with him and that he was going to take a shower at the hospital. I don't want to arrive at the dinner too early without my date. I should have just told him I could pick him up. I'll leave the house when he's leaving the hospital; that way we can probably arrive at the same time.*

"May I speak to Dr. Richard Thomas?" asked Tina.

"One moment please," said the receptionist.

*I don't like calling his cell when he's working. I always catch him with a patient. I prefer to call his office.*

"Dr. Thomas speaking; may I help you?"

"Yes, I need a complete rub down from head to toe, and afterwards I need a good fuck," laughed Tina.

"Baby, you're nasty," smiled Richard through the phone.

I knew he'd really gotten attached to me over the last few weeks. He really enjoyed my company.

"Baby, what time do you think you'll be leaving?" I asked him.

"I'm finishing up with my last patient. I should be leaving in about thirty minutes—after I shower and change," said Dr. Thomas.

"Okay, I'll leave my house in half-an-hour. Hopefully, we'll meet up at the same time. Don't forget the address and directions I gave you."

"I left your note with the directions in the car. I'll see you in thirty," said Dr. Thomas. We hung up.

*I wonder what Tracy is up to. She didn't want to go to the dinner at first. She was so fucking mad at Rock over what had happened at Chili's. I can't blame her; he totally disrespected her. I'm glad I was able to talk her into going. I told her, we all needed to get out together again. It should be fun.*

*Ding, dong, ding, dong.*

*Who the hell is ringing my door bell now? This is happening a little too much.*

"Yes?" I asked.

"Package for Tina Baker." Said the IPS delivery man

"I'm Tina Baker."

"Please sign here."

I signed; he handed me the package and left.

*I wasn't expecting any delivery. I know I didn't order anything. The return address is a local P.O Box here in Michigan. I wonder who this is from.*

I opened the package and extracted a DVD. *I wonder what this is about.* But, in the back of my mind, I knew what the DVD contained. I loaded the disk in the DVD player and pushed "play."

As soon as I saw what was playing on the DVD, I fainted.

# Chapter 31

## The Dinner Party

Tamika held out her hand to G. G pushed her hand away and hugged her. Jason stood back, watching, as the pair embraced. G hollered for Tim to come to the door.

"Tim, I need you here. You will never believe who is standing on your threshold," hollered G, smiling at Tamika.

Jason decided to cut in. "Okay, how do you know Tamika?" he asked, staring at G as if he were crazy.

"We attended the same college," said G, still smiling.

When Tim saw Tamika, he instantly walked up to her, and grabbed her up, hugging her. Everybody started talking over each other; you could barely understand what they were saying. Jason was just as confused as Lisa, who was standing in the background looking at all the commotion. Tim, G, and Tamika were asking each other what they had been up to since they left college. Lisa cut into the conversation by extending her hand and introducing herself to Tamika.

"I'm sorry baby; this is Tamika; we attended U&A," Tim introduced. "Tamika this is my lovely wife, Lisa."

"We already met. You and G were so busy running your mouth that I introduced myself," said Lisa.

They all stood at the doorway of the house for over fifteen minutes, just reminiscing about their college days. Everyone was smiling and laughing until G and Tim, looked over at Jason.

"Why ya'll niggas looking at me like that?" asked Jason.

"She didn't tell you?" asked G.

"Tell me what? And who is *she*?" asked Jason.

"Tamika," said G, looking at Tamika for a response.

Tamika cut in and asked, "What was I supposed to tell Jason?"

"Please tell me, you know who Jason is related to" said G.

"No, I don't know who Jason is related too. I know he has an older brother," said Tamika, but he doesn't really talk about him much.

Tim and G looked at each other and decided to ask Jason the same question.

"Jason, you didn't tell Tamika who your big brother is?" asked G.

"Yes, I told her I had an older brother and that he was locked up," said Jason.

"Did you tell her who your older brother was? Like, did you happen to mention his name?" asked G.

"No, his name didn't matter at the time. Why?" asked Jason.

Tamika had a puzzled look on her face now. She didn't like where this conversation was going. She could feel the tension rising in the air. Knots were forming in her stomach. If what she was thinking was true, her relationship with Jason might be over.

Tim couldn't keep up the suspense any longer. "Jason, Tamika used to date your brother in college," he explained, standing back to take in everybody's reaction.

Jason looked at Tamika; there was hurt written all over his face. He couldn't believe what he'd just heard. The only thought going through his mind now was.

*Is Mike her daughter's father, and am I Sya's uncle?*

Tamika put her hand up to her mouth—just as shocked as Jason was. She put a hand on Jason's shoulder, trying to explain that she didn't know Mike was his brother. Tears were streaming down her face. She never thought in a million years that this would happen. The man she had grown to love over a few weeks was about to walk out of her life. They both stood there together, looking at each other with a hurt look in their eyes.

The reality of what had come to light made Jason see that he was in love with Tamika, but he was stung by the fact that Mike might be her daughter's father. He needed to know the truth.

The room was quiet; no one said a word. Tim, G and Lisa understood that something was up, but they could only watch as two lovers' hearts were being torn apart.

# Chapter 32

**Tracy**

"Tracy, you ready to go?" Rock hollered to me up the stairs.

"I'm coming," I hollered back.

"You've been in the bathroom for over thirty minutes. I'm ready to go; I'm hungry as hell. I hope they got some fried wingdings," said Rock, rubbing his stomach.

"Listen to your greedy ass," I teased, coming down the stairs: "just like a nigga. Can't wait to go eat for free."

"Damn baby, you look good as hell. We're just going over to Tim and Lisa's house. You didn't have to put on that dress."

"Am I overdressed?" I asked, looking down at my attire.

"Yes...you see, I have on jeans and a sweater. The invitation said, come casual and comfortable, not dressy."

"I didn't even read the invitation. I knew we were going to dinner at their house. I figured it was dressy, here, let me slip into some jeans."

"Hurry up!" said Rock.

********************************

"I'm ready, let's bounce," I said.

I enjoyed my conversation with Rock on the way to Tim and Lisa's house. We hadn't had a decent conversation since we'd had that altercation at Chili's. It felt good to have a normal conversation without arguing.

"We're here," said Rock.

"That was fast, I didn't pay attention to the time because we were talking."

I felt like coming clean with Rock about the abortion. But I didn't know if now would be a good time. We were finally getting along, and I didn't want to spoil the evening. I decided to just let it go.

# Chapter 33

## The Dinner Party

Before they could ring the doorbell, Tim was opening the door.

"What up, my nigga?" said Tim. "I saw you pulling up."

"I'm straight and hungry," laughed Rock.

"Nigga, you *always* hungry," said Tim.

"I guess ya'll so busy, ya'll forgot about me," said Tracy.

"I'm sorry, baby," said Tim, hugging Tracy. "How have you been doing?"

"I'm doing great. Where's my girl?" asked Tracy, looking around for Lisa.

"She's in the kitchen," said Rock.

"Well, I'm going to see if Lisa needs any help," said Tracy, heading for the kitchen.

"You will never guess who's here," Tim told Rock after Tracy left.

"Who?" asked Rock, frowning up at Tim, wondering who he could be talking about.

"Tamika."

"Are you talking about Tamika Jones? Mike's old girlfriend from U&A?"

"Yep. But guess who ol' girl came with," said Tim, looking excited. He couldn't wait to tell Rock.

"Who, man?"

"Jason."

"Hell naw!" hollered Rock in disbelief.

"He didn't even know she used to date Mike, and *she* didn't know he was Mike's brother."

"Damn, that's fucked up," said Rock.

"I know. Man, they look like they're in love," Tim confided.

"Damn!" said Rock. The news shocked him.

"They're downstairs in the basement talking now," said Tim.

"I hope everything works out," said Rock.

"I don't know, man, Jason looked real hurt," said Tim.

"We'll see. —Right now I need an ice cold brew," said Rock, pushing past Tim, looking for the beer.

"Okay. They're in the cooler in the family room" said Tim.

*********************************

Lisa and Tracy could be heard talking and laughing in the kitchen, catching up on old times. They hadn't seen each other since Tracy had gotten discharged from the hospital.

"It smells good in here," said Tracy.

"Well I hope you brought a big appetite. I have a buffet spread," said Lisa.

"Hey, I'm ready. And I know my greedy-ass husband is. That's all he was talking about on the way here," said Tracy.

"Well, go make yourself comfortable, and I'll be in there in a minute," said Lisa.

"Okay. Let me know if you need help with anything," said Tracy, walking out of the kitchen.

She bumped into Rock and Tim in the hallway.

"G's in the family room with his date. Let's go in there until the food is ready," suggested Tim.

Through the doorway of the family room, they could see G standing in front of the tv, playing bowling on the Wii game. His date was sitting with her back to everyone.

"What up, nigga?" hollered Rock.

G, turned around, saw Rock and Tracy, and came over and gave them a hug.

"I want you to meet my friend Alexis," said G.

When the name Alexis spilled from G's lips, Rock froze in place; he didn't take another step.

Alexis stood up, came around the couch, extended her hand to Rock, with a smirk on her face.

Tracy instantly stepped in front of Rock and smacked the shit out of Alexis.

All hell broke loose.

# Chapter 34

## Dr. Richard Thomas

*I'm getting worried. Tina's not answering her cell phone. I think I'll go by her house just to be safe.*

\*\*\*\*\*\*\*\*\*\*\*\*\*\*\*\*\*\*\*\*\*\*\*\*\*\*\*\*\*\*\*\*\*\*\*\*\*\*\*\*

*Her car is still parked in the driveway. Maybe she fell asleep. She not's answering her door.*

I began pounding on the door, still no answer. I kept hitting the door harder and harder until, finally, I heard movement in the house. "Tina!" I cried; "Tina!"

Tina came to the door, holding her forehead.

"Baby, what happened?" I asked.

"I think I fainted," said Tina. I could see she was trying to compose herself.

"Come over here and lie on the couch. Let me take a look at you."

"I'm okay; it's just a little bump" said Tina, stumbling toward the couch. "I'm all right.

"You don't look all right. What made you faint? Is there something wrong?"

"Just something I have to take care of."

"Are you still up to going to the dinner?" I asked with concern.

"Yes, Dr. Thomas, I'm okay" smiled Tina, trying to compose herself. She had a lovely smile—even with a bump on her head.

# Chapter 35

**Tina**

I kept that smile plastered on my face. I tried not to show Richard my real emotions.

I was truly worried. The recording on the DVD showed me performing sex acts I would never voluntarily do. My eyes were closed the whole time. You could tell I was not aware of what was going on.

The DVD showed Alexis engaging in oral sex with me. I looked as if I were enjoying what Alexis was doing; however, I never once opened my eyes. My body seemed to be in a limp state.

After Alexis finished her cunnilingus, she took a couple of dildos from a bag and used them on me. She must have kept at it for a good half-hour. I couldn't believe what I was seeing on the tape. How could she stoop to doing something like this. What did I do to deserve this I kept asking myself.

I couldn't imagine what Alexis wanted to use the tape for. I was going to come clean about it with Richard. I didn't want to start off a relationship with skeletons in my closet. I didn't want him to be Stuck in the Dark about me. I planned on telling him after we came back to my place after the dinner.

"You ready to go?" asked Richard, pulling me out of my daydream

"Yes, let's go."

\*\*\*\*\*\*\*\*\*\*\*\*\*\*\*\*\*\*\*\*\*\*\*\*\*\*\*\*\*\*\*\*\*\*\*\*\*\*\*\*\*

"Are you ready for this?" asked Richard, as he pulled up to Tim and Lisa's house

"Ready for what?" I asked.

"I know you haven't told your friends you're dating a white boy," smiled Richard.

"Who cares? I'm a grown-ass woman," I declared, kissing Richard passionately before we got out of the car.

As we approached the door, we could hear hollering and fussing inside the house.

"Damn, what's going on in there?" I wondered, ringing the door bell, and, when nobody responded, I started banging on the door.

"Sounds like somebody is fighting. You sure you want to go in there?" asked Richard.

"Those are my friends in there; something is definitely wrong," I told him, banging on the door even harder.

Finally, Lisa came to the door looking exhausted and upset.

"Lisa, what's going on?" I asked her.

"Tracy and G's date were fighting," said Lisa.

"What?" I said, looking at Lisa like she was speaking a foreign language.

"I don't know what's going on, but apparently G's date knows Rock," said Lisa.

"Is that the woman Tracy was telling me about who whispered in Rock's ear?" I wondered.

"Whispered in Rock's ear?" asked Lisa, shocked.

"Where's Tracy? I need to check on my girl," I said, barging in.

"Tracy's in our bedroom with Rock and Tim. They're trying to calm her down, and G's date is in our guest room with G," said Lisa.

Rushing toward the bedroom to check on Tracy, I had forgot to introduce Richard to Lisa. "Lisa I'm sorry; this is Dr. Richard Thomas, my date," I hollered over my shoulder.

"How do you do?" said Richard politely, over *his* shoulder, running to keep up with me.

*****************************************

With Richard at my heels, I burst into the bedroom and ran up to Tracy, hugging her, trying to calm her down. Rock was looking at Richard, wondering who this white guy was.

"Tracy, what happened?" asked Tina.

"That bitch we saw at the restaurant. She's here with G," cried Tracy.

"Oh, hell naw!" I couldn't believe it.

Poor Richard stood back observing all the commotion. I bet he had never experienced anything like this.

Tracy and I got up together and headed for the guest room. Rock tried to stop us, but he knew it was a lost cause. We had already made up our minds.

I banged on the guest-room door. "Bitch, open up!"

The door opened. Nothing could have prepared me for the person who appeared on the other side. Alexis stood there smiling at me.

I didn't think twice; Tracy and I charged into Alexis like football players, slamming her into the wall. G came from behind, grabbed me, and lifting me up in the air.

Alexis started laughing like a crazy woman. Everyone turned their attention to her. She pointed to all of us, all the while spilling her guts out. She told everything.

After Alexis finished blabbing her announcement of sorts, we all sat down in the family room in shock. We couldn't believe the information Alexis had laid out for them. Lisa stood there looking at all of us in total disbelief.

# Chapter 36

## Tamika

We sat in the basement, Jason and I, just looking at each other, not knowing what to say. Finally, I broke the silence.

"I'm so sorry, Jason, I had no idea Mike was your brother," I sobbed.

"I know, I've thought about it, and I can't blame you."

"What are we going to do now?"

"First, I need to know: who is your daughter's father?"

I lowered my head. I knew the answer would hurt Jason, but I didn't want to lie to him. "Your brother, Mike," I said. I looked at him.

"I knew it. I understand now why you didn't tell him. My brother has always been a hothead and only thinks of himself. He was full of himself when he was in college," said Jason.

"That's why I just kept it to myself and went on with my life. I was going to have an abortion because I knew I wanted to go to medical school. My mother told me not to worry about it, God takes care of babies and fools. I can't thank my mother enough. I'm so glad I kept my baby. Now I have a beautiful daughter."

"And I have a beautiful niece," said Jason, looking in my eyes.

"I'm going to tell your brother."

"No, let me. I'm going to tell him how he missed out on a beautiful woman, and I'm glad he did. Because, if he didn't, I wouldn't have you now," said Jason.

He took me in his arms and pressed me to his chest. I knew I had finally found true love.

We sat like that while all the commotion was going on upstairs. A couple of times, I thought we should investigate, but Jason didn't want to let me go. After a while, we made our way up stairs and came across a roomful of individuals who looked like they had been through hell.

"What the hell happened up here?" asked Jason.

"Everything!" shouted Lisa, standing in the doorway of the family room, crying.

# Chapter 37

**Tracy**

I sat there with tears streaming down my face. Alexis had informed everyone that she and Rock were fucking. My heart was on fire, aching from the hurt of knowing that my husband had been sleeping with another woman. He hadn't taken our wedding vows seriously. I sat there, holding my chest thinking back to the last time I caught Rock cheating on me. I thought I would never get over it. I cried for days. I sat down and wrote a poem filled with the heartache I was experiencing.

*Heartache!*

My heart is aching, can't you tell?
My stomach is in knots, going through a
    love spell.

This man of mine, is driving me crazy.
The room seems small, dark and hazy.

I don't like this feeling deep down in my
    heart,
How could loving someone tear me a-part?

My feelings run deep, so deep you
    wouldn't understand.
This human form I keep seeing resembles
    a man—

Someone I thought ached for me the same
    way,
But I learned that he's different; I learned
    the hard way.

Don't love someone more than you love
    yourself,
Put the man up above in your heart; he
    knows what you felt.

He comforts you in the darkest hours,
Lights up your life with sunshine and
    flowers.

Gwen Cannon

Look in the mirror—who do you see?
Someone reaching out for comfort. That
someone is me.

# Chapter 38

### The Dinner Party

Now everyone was in total shock. Richard held on to Tina. She just stood there shaking. Tracy was sitting over by the window, crying and holding her chest. Rock kept trying to hold her, but, every time he touched her, she would try to slap the shit out of him. G, just stood there staring at everybody. He couldn't believe he had been dating Alexis for two weeks and didn't have a clue that she was crazy as hell.

"You are a crazy-ass bitch," hollered G.

"Yeah, I'm crazy, and your friends are fucked up. I ran game on you and your boy. I fucked both of y'all. Let me see who fucked the best," laughed Alexis.

"You know what? Your ass is crazy as hell, just like your fucking brother. That's why I shot his stupid ass," Rock blurted out.

The room went silent. Everybody looked at Rock. Tracy got up and walked over to him. She couldn't believe what she had heard.

"*You* killed Chris?" cried Tracy, looking at Rock like he was a stranger.

"Yeah, and I don't regret that shit. He tried to kill *you*, baby. I couldn't let that shit just pass," said Rock, looking to the rest of his friends for understanding.

No one noticed Alexis leave the room. When she came back, she held a gun in her hand.

She told Tim, Lisa, Jason, Tamika, Richard, and G to leave the room. She herded them into the basement. Once they went downstairs, Alexis locked the door. They kept trying to convince her to put the gun down, but she wasn't listening. She had put her plan into place months ago, right after her brother died. She just needed to know who was involved and how. Now she knew. Rock was the killer— as she'd suspected all along (that's why she'd screwed him, to pump him for information)—and, as far as she was concerned, Tracy and Tina were just as guilty for covering up for him and treating Chris badly when he was alive. That's why she gave Tina a taste of the down-low thang, and now she was about to give all three of them a taste of death!

Tracy, Tina, and Rock stood in the middle of the room shaking like fucking leaves. They were begging her to let them go, that she would go to jail.

"Alexis, please let us go," begged Rock.

"Shut the fuck up! You just admitted you killed my brother!" screamed Alexis.

"Let Tina and Tracy go. They didn't' have anything to do with this," Rock tried to convince Alexis.

Alexis shoved the barrel of the gun right under Rock's nose. "What the fuck do I care about those two bitches, tryin' to beat me up every chance they got? They deserve to die, too!"

Tina was waiting for her chance. When Alexis got up in Rock's face, Tina took off running out of the room. Alexis came right after her.

# Chapter 39

**Tina**

The escalating sound of gunshots and screams could be heard throughout the house. I started running away from the gun fire. My only thought was to try to get the hell out there as fast as possible. But before I could make it to the door, I felt an intense burning sensation. My back felt like as if someone had taken a blow torch to it. I fell face forward on the floor.

I lay there with tears streaming down my face, I couldn't move. I felt as if a ton of bricks were stacked on top of my back. I could hear footsteps, coming closer and closer—a woman's footstep; I could tell by the heels tapping on the floor. I lay there pretending to be dead.

As she walked around me, saying, "You little bitch," I could hear sirens in the distance; someone must have heard the commotion and called the police. *Please, Lord, hurry up, and let this bitch go on her way. I don't want to die.* It felt like hours, but I knew it only had been seconds stretching into minutes.

My back was soaking wet; I knew it was from my blood. How much was I losing? I didn't have a clue. I started feeling cold; I was losing consciousness.

As I lay there on the floor, I thought of all the shit I had tucked away in my closet, deep dark secrets no one even knew.

# Chapter 40

### Tina – the Aftermath

I woke up to a light shining in my face. *Am I in heaven?* I thought. The light went away, but my vision was blurred. I was trying to make out the figure in front of me. The voice sounded familiar, but I still couldn't make out who it was.

"Tina, can you hear me?" asked Dr. Thomas.

My voice was raspy and dry. "Yes. Where am I?"

"You're in the hospital," said Dr. Thomas.

"How long?"

"Five days. ...Tina, can you feel this?" He was sticking my feet with a pen. I couldn't feel anything. I started panicking,

I couldn't feel my legs. I kept grabbing my leg, but I didn't have any feeling in them. I broke down crying, I knew I couldn't walk.

"Tina, calm down," soothed Dr. Thomas, holding Tina close to his chest.

I tried to compose myself. I asked him what happened to Tracy and Rock. I could tell from his expression it wasn't good.

I lay there, tears running down my face. He explained everything that happened that night. Tracy and Rock were shot and killed. Alexis was arrested for their deaths. Tim, Lisa, Jason, G, and Tamika were okay. I was numb; I had lost my best friend. I could have saved her if I had gone to the police in the beginning. I stood there and watched Rock shoot Chris in the court house, and I didn't say shit. I tucked that shit away in the closet, and look what it cost me: my best friend and her husband. I wanted to die.

# Epilogue

Jason went to visit his brother in prison. As he explained to Tamika, he felt that he should be the one to break the news to his brother that he had a daughter.

Mike was happy and sad at the same time. He never had the chance to see his daughter as a little child, and now he wouldn't get the chance to see her grow up. He asked Jason to send him a picture of his daughter.

Mike understood why Jason had fallen in love with Tamika. She was a good woman. Mike knew that he had never really appreciated the  fact that Tamkia was a good woman when they were together.  Mike had been selfish and young and didn't think about anyone else but himself.

Tamika held off telling Sya who her father was. She didn't know how she would react, knowing her father was in prison for killing someone.

Tim and Lisa are happily awaiting the arrival of their baby boy. Yeah, they found out it's a boy.

G—he left Detroit, and moved out to Atlanta. He said he couldn't take any more of the drama; he almost lost his life. He opened up a strip club, named Booty-Licous. They say, it's the hottest strip club in Atlanta.

As for me, I'm going to physical therapy to learn how to walk all over again. I have the best therapist in Detroit—uh-huh: Dr. Richard Thomas, my husband. I couldn't have asked for a better man.

# About the Author

Gwen Cannon was born and raised in the Jefferies Housing Projects, located in Detroit, Michigan. Her motivation to survive, and not to become a product of her environment is what drove her ambition to succeed. She currently reside in Dearborn, Michigan with her husband James Cannon, and their five sons, James Jr, Corey, Jonathan, Jordan, Jalen and one granddaughter, CoMya.

She would like to leave her readers with this note, *(Take control of your life, don't let the individuals in your life take control of you!) Don't place blame on the people in your life, you are what you become.*

If you would like to know more about Gwen Cannon, please visit her website at www.gwencannon.net.

Be sure to check out these books
by Gwen Cannon:
**Everything that looks good, ain't good for
you!**

**Stuck in the Dark**

**Scandalous**

Order online at, Barnes and Noble, and
Amazon.com

# Coming Soon

Caught up!